BORGIAS

DBC Pierre has worked as a designer and cartoonist, and currently lives in Ireland. His first novel, *Vernon God Little*, won the 2003 Bollinger Everyman Wodehouse Award, the 2004 Whitbread Prize for Best First Novel, and the 2003 Man Booker Prize, and is sold in forty-three countries.

His relationship with Hammer stretches back to earliest childhood. He describes never having been so chilled and intrigued as with the supernatural Hammer films he grew up with. Their effect was so great that he spent many schooldays drawing replica storyboards on cash-register rolls, and holding showings for classmates on a shoe-box cinema.

'If any novelist can collate the killing irony of what is happening around us, it is DBC Pierre'
Guardian

'Winningly peculiar'
Independent

'A thoroughly modern nightmare . . . DBC Pierre stacks up the layers of horror with relish and skill – the Hammer label gives him a perfect excuse to leave no stop unpulled'
The Times

Also by DBC Pierre

Vernon God Little
Ludmila's Broken English
Lights Out in Wonderland
Petit Mal

BREAKFAST
WITH THE
BORGIAS

DBC PIERRE

FP
2/15

AN EXCLUSIVE MEDIA COMPANY

Published by Arrow Books in association with Hammer 2015

2 4 6 8 10 9 7 5 3 1

First published in Great Britain in 2014 by
Arrow Books in association with Hammer

Random House, 20 Vauxhall Bridge Road
London SW1V 2SA

www.randomhouse.co.uk

Addresses for companies within The Random House Group Limited can be
found at: www.randomhouse.co.uk/offices.htm

The Random House Group Limited Reg. No. 954009

A CIP catalogue record for this book
is available from the British Library

ISBN 9780099586241

Typeset in Centaur MT (13.5/16pt) by Palimpsest Book Production Ltd,
Falkirk, Stirlingshire
Printed and bound by CPI Group (UK) Ltd, Croydon, CR0 4YY

MIX
Paper from
responsible sources
FSC
www.fsc.org   FSC® C018179

Penguin Random House is committed to a sustainable
future for our business, our readers and our planet.
This book is made from Forest Stewardship Council®
certified paper.

ACT ONE

I

Technology is the way, the truth and the life. Nobody comes to the light except through it. Algorithms are the new DNA, and just as well: because today the race is to the swift, the battle is to the strong, and time and chance happeneth not to them.

But the clock over platform four was analogue. Its second hand was red. On the tip a disc juddered like a wrecking ball smacking granite. As if time didn't want to pass. Still, it did crumble past until finally, at nine forty-eight this November eve, Zeva Neely had four minutes left for her phone to ring; or something was badly wrong.

She held it like a prayer book in her small gloved hands. It looked as if it had never rung before. Despite this lack of news it kissed her face with light, and that promise alone was enough to fix her to the screen. Perhaps because underneath lived anything important she had ever said or heard, she flicked through that history looking for clues about today. They were in a month-long conversation that had ended abruptly yesterday. Her chat was green and his was white, on a wallpaper of hearts and dynamite:

ARI: If you trust me what's the problem?

ZEV: Oh now it's date rape, thanks.

ARI: You said you would like it too.

ZEV: Don't tell me what I said, Ariel.

She shivered. Bruxelles-Midi station was glacial. If the device didn't ring or flash a message before her train arrived she would shatter inside. She shouldn't even board. She started to wish the train had struck a bridge. Stiff as a mouse among pigeons, peering through her fringe at this wrong place to be, wrong people teeming, a horse-yard of breath lit by screens, she was tugged at by every one of the three thousand, four hundred and seventy miles she was from home. She knew the distance exactly, having looked it up on her computer, confirmed it on her tablet, double-checked it with GPS, and sent the data to her phone to use against him.

The screen's radiance lured her back:

ARI: I don't get it. It's not like you.

ZEV: Don't pull my damned strings.

ARI: But what is the exact problem?

ZEV: Someone will recognise me.

ARI: Dress different. They won't expect undergrads.

ZEV: Now you're saying I'm ordinary.

She quickly rebooted the phone in case messages had jammed between countries. The screen died and shone again, but nothing new arrived.

She returned to her message history:

ARI: Calculate how much risk this is.

ZEV: That's what I'm saying, duh.

ARI: I mean the risk is all mine. An undergrad
       with a faculty member has no problem.
       A professor with an undergrad has a
       problem.

ZEV: Uh-huh, you're the adult and I'm the child.

ARI: Zeva. Let's do this, come on – but elegantly.

The platform jangled. Three minutes to hope the train had broken down. If only he would call, send a message, she would leap aboard before it even stopped. But the list of bad omens inflated fast. She clung to only one of them – that she should have worn a hoodie. A hoodie isn't a garment but a cabin that you wear. And this meatspace was no place to be exposed. She ducked under echoes and hunched into her coat. Usually she wore earphones; now they were too scary, her favourite tunes were as taunting as lullabies played to a murder. All because something was wrong.

ZEV: *It's mid semester. I don't even have a passport. And you give Intro to Algorithms the week you say we're in Europe. It's crazy.*

ARI: *One of our tickets is paid. Let's not waste it. The conference is easy, you be a tourist in the day, and we meet at night. Then later – us alone. More freedom than here.*

ZEV: *Here will be taking multiple-choice to decide if I went as your student, assistant or sex slave. And what do I tell my folks?*

ARI: *That you're twenty-three.*

ZEV: *Bye, Pa, dirty week in Europe with the associate professor. My grades need it.*

ARI: *If you mean am I serious, I am serious. I want to be with you.*

She pictured him, brooding falcon of a man

under the hood of his duffel coat. They were a couple of the future, of the mind alone, untethered to cumbersome flesh. After meeting in an online tutorial, the page of her life had merged with his.

Ariel Panek. Wunderkind. Sophomore magnet. Barely thirty.

He had something. Vision. Correct thinking given that the entire human race would fit into a grape if you sucked the space out of its atoms. It fell to them to aim for that shimmer and run there. It was a pact. The future. And she did head that way, spontaneously, unquestioningly. They had found each other headed there.

Together into post-human times.

Two minutes to hope the train was derailed. She glanced up the platform. Mist iced the distance into smoke. Wires and tracks cut skate marks to infinity.

ZEV: *Isn't it just tacky? Like the manager and his cashier at some motel?*

ARI: *It's an adventure.*

ZEV: Two adventures. It's one adventure if we
travel together.

ARI: We fly back together. The Cloud Servers
team and some of the AI lab will be at the
conference. I got a later flight, I think alone,
but we still can't risk the airport together,
delegates will be everywhere. Later the
world can be ours.

ZEV: Yours maybe, you're the European. I never
went further than Chicago and that was
stressful as hell.

ARI: I want to give you the world. Want you to eat
it. Watch it function. Human systems,
remember it's also research. And your room
in Brussels can be at the airport, the train is
right there. I'll meet you next night at the
station in Amsterdam.

ZEV: And if the flights get messed up? Or the
train? Or if I don't find you?

ARI: Come on – in the new world? How many

ways do we have to be in touch? Seven?
Eight? I'll let you know the second I land, or
you don't have to get on the train. And to
find me is easy – the one in the hood.

Ariel understood the hoodie. They had it in common. His almost never came down, even indoors, even in summer. He knew that earphones made it a bedroom and the passing world a movie. With shades it was a party where the only guest was you. And it wasn't just taste. He had an ethic. The hoodie wasn't fashion but a way forward in our time. Whatever made outside more virtual made inside more real; and for him the real was under his hood in his head, running clean.

She loved this. Believed in it. Clean running.

One minute to pray the train had hit a cow. She cuddled the screen to her chest, cocking from side to side to keep her breath from frosting it.

ARI: *This is one hard honeymoon to sell.*

ZEV: *Honeymoon? You skipped Vegas.*

ARI: *You know what I mean. Why are you so hard to convince?*

ZEV: *Why are you so determined to convince me?*

A man approached Zeva and spoke in a rasping language. She flinched and moved to a lonely space at the end of the platform. Suddenly she was the foreign one, too shiny with her coat, her brooch, her matching luggage. She was a beacon that flashed *America*, that hollered *Jacqueline Kennedy lost her hat*. Zeva was a girl who hid at parties if she went at all. Now she was a cake in a window. In clothes she didn't like or understand, waiting to know if someone who couldn't match socks was going to show.

Her fatal flaw: romance. No scale of algorithm could fix it.

Unlike the dead whose bodies get lighter when they're gone, her screen grew heavier the more she stared at it. With adrenalin and pain. With messages from all the Zevas before this one. The young dumb one.

She wiped a sleeve across her face. Glanced up at the clock. It was nine fifty-two. Departure time.

If she boarded she would have to blame her tears on the chill. Anyway, her features were of a dewy type, already shiny at the edges, red-nosed in the cold.

Loudspeakers boomed: 'Amsterdam.' Headlights gleamed down the line.

A breeze flew up. Tracks began to hum.

Her message timeline reached yesterday:

ARI: Wait until Amsterdam. First night in a suite. I
       want you to feel like Princess Leia. A butler
       can take our picture.

ZEV: Butler? Should've packed a tennis skirt.
       Listen, buddy, you better be at that station.
       It's an old war movie already. Seriously
       promise me.

ARI: I promise. Don't worry. I'm a few hours
       behind you.

She clung to that message. Kept it open on her screen.

After all, they were in a pact. Only they would be standing at the end of the story. The new world wasn't fashion, it was survival. Clean algorithms were its alchemy.

Ariel Panek was her code. The algorithmist.

The train slid past like a burrowing worm, growling, hissing, peeing fluids, making sounds of unstoppable mass, to her those forces had their sounds.

She clasped her stomach as it clanked to a stop.

2

The sound of slowing turbines still whistled under Ariel's hood — and now their sinking whine described his day. 'I think we should turn back.' He pulled a bag on to his lap. 'I don't have a good feeling. Better to wait at the airport. If things get worse I could be stuck out here.' He checked the time. It was eight fifty-two in the evening.

That meant nine fifty-two in Brussels. Zeva would be boarding her train.

'If things get any worse,' said the driver, 'we'll be kipping in the car. Never seen anything like it. Global warming, they say. Well, I wouldn't bloody mind if it actually got any warmer. My godfathers, look at it! Never mind diverting planes, at least they've got instruments. I can barely see the bonnet of me bloody car.'

Like crabs and carcasses tossed up in a sea storm, Ariel's essences flashed into view. For one thing, you could see he was a swimmer. His forte was butterfly stroke, he defaulted to that power unconsciously. Because as the last street lamp fell behind them, his arms rose to his shoulders and floated there, ready to thresh.

Puttering around a bend there came a thump from outside.

'Welcome to Suffolk,' said the driver. 'Bloody typical.'

'Wo! Did we kill him?' Ariel pressed his nose to the window.

'Put it this way: he will have felt better.' The man threw his head back to laugh, a bray that was starting to irritate. '*Ma-a-a-a.*'

'Seriously: let's go back. I can pay. I mean, we're starting to hit wildlife. I didn't think it would be so far. It's ridiculous.'

'Not unusual, pheasants on these little roads.' The driver peered back through the mirror. 'They don't fly high enough. And they're slow off the ground.'

Ariel pulled out his phone and tapped the screen. Still no signal. He should have tried at the airport, but the time between the flight and now had somehow been a blur, almost something dreamt rather than lived. Such was his excitement, he supposed. Such was his stress. It had seemed logical to wait ten minutes for privacy and quiet.

He should have stayed there. With networks, reason and roasted coffee.

The screen lit his scowl like a crystal ball. He opened a crack in the window, wincing through a blast of cold with a stench of rotting leaves. Scanning the night air with the phone barely made the signal quiver for an instant, and then die.

'Seriously,' he said. 'We need to turn back.'

'Ordinarily, sir, the world'd be your oyster – but the A road's shut behind us now, remember all those flashing lights? We were lucky to get this far, God knows what's gone on. Must be an accident back near the airport. Listen to my radio, there's no other cabs about. I'll drop you then crawl home meself.'

Ariel slumped in his seat. Now the seat covers

irritated him. The pine deodoriser, the hiss of the radio, the snack debris. In fact the car must have been forty years old if it was a day. He couldn't understand how it could still be a licensed taxi. All this added to his discomfort. His skin felt coated in a traveller's gel, part congealed sweat, part static electricity. He could smell himself.

And outside was grey and deadly still. When he gazed into the fog all it showed was a universe made of particles, and tonight they had frosted to a halt.

Ariel flicked through all his social pages, his messaging, mail and chat; but they were rooms after a party, flotsam from an alien mood and time.

Happening upon yesterday's chat, his brow fell:

ARI: Wait until Amsterdam. First night in a suite. I want you to feel like Princess Leia. A butler can take our picture.

ZEV: Butler? Should've packed a tennis skirt. Listen, buddy, you better be at that station. It's an old war movie already. Seriously promise me.

ARI: *I promise. Don't worry. I'm a few hours*
    behind you.

Ariel caught the driver's eye. 'Could we at least stop while I try to make a call? I'm seriously losing connectivity.'

'Connectivity,' mused the driver. 'There's a word for you. When I was a nipper it would've meant Lego. *Ma-a-a.* But honestly, I can't even see the verge. In these conditions your best bet's the hotel. Not too far now.'

'But if you see a place? I would really thank you.'

The car hummed on. Each twig and pebble it touched, every roll of its wheels echoed crackling off the mist like a beast's first footfall on earth.

The phone jangled to life on the incline of a hill. Ariel snatched it up.

The line was dead before it reached his hood.

He redialled twice in vain before reaching to squeeze the driver's shoulder: 'What was that last big town? Can we just go there? I could connect, find something to eat – I didn't even take out any local currency. You could just leave me there, in fact.'

'Ipswich? Far behind us I'm afraid. I mean, not so far as the crow flies. But there won't be any crows up tonight. You sit tight, sir — from what I recall it's a seaside resort they've booked you. You'll soon be in your jacuzzi, all connected up like a Christmas tree.'

The phone switched from *Emergency Calls Only* to *No Network* as they coasted downhill. It still threw up a halo, made him a virtual saint in its glow; but the glow was empty. A moment later it fell dark. Ariel looked around at twenty kilograms of modern luggage — two laptops, a tablet, three kilos of cables and drives, and an Android device.

Each contained nothing less than his life.

All were precisely useless.

For some reason it invoked his mother's voice: *Like you were even going to call,* she said in that tone of hers, as flat as a vaudeville comedian. *Like I mean something to you.*

His gaze drifted to a snapshot clipped to the dashboard. In it the driver wore a crooked smile and rested one fat arm around a lanky girl of about ten. Her hair was cut like a boy's, she wore dirty dungarees; and a fish dangled at the end of a rod beside her runaway grin. The picture made her a son the driver never had. It stirred something in Ariel, scooped a bone from somewhere in his bubbling stock of stress and fatigue. The feeling wasn't warm. To the contrary, it brought a chill. Somehow he realised that his depths had nothing to do with circuits or algorithms. His fatal weakness was people. In all their crooked, runaway, fat-armed wonder.

'Someone expecting you?' asked the driver.

'Not out here. I'm going to a conference. My girlfriend's already there.'

'Oh? Congratulations. Nice little perk, dragging the missus along. Not that I'd want mine around, if you know what I mean. *Ma-a-a.*'

'We're in the same field.'

'And what field might that be, if you don't mind me asking?'

'AI,' said Ariel. 'I mean – computer science.'

'AI? Don't tell me – the "I" must stand for international. Well, not much of a clue, I can hear you're from overseas.'

'Artificial intelligence.' Ariel let his head fall back. He closed his eyes, trying to warm himself with positive thoughts. For one thing, according to the driver he was at least bound for a major hotel. There he would seize back the day. There, over a burger and fries, with a coffee and some Wi-Fi, he would wrest back control.

His arms fell limp at his sides.

'Artificial intelligence? What we at the rugby club call *beer*. *Ma-a-a-a*. Mind you, doesn't work on everyone.'

Ariel sunk lower. He stared ahead into a furnace of boiling frost thrown by the headlights. Plans raced through his mind for the hotel: find nearby airports, braver taxis, send supper, flowers, champagne to her room.

'Still, that's interesting,' the driver went on. 'So I mean, in your expert opinion – will computers really ever replace human beings?'

'Not a question of replacing. More of joining.'

'No, no, I know – but do you think they'll ever match, you know, the way we think and so forth? Like what we call our humanity?'

'Why not? The brain is a processor, after all.'

'But how can I put it: life's rich tapestry and all that. Like just now you said, "I don't have a good feeling" – they won't ever get that far?'

'Oh sure. Instinct is just a scan of previous outcomes. Not such a big deal. Up to now our only real obstacle has been processing power.'

'Is that all we are? Processing power? Blimey.'

'We don't need more. In the end we're all the same, we just learn to chase the good.'

The car crunched over gravel, slowing as the driver checked his bearings. 'Well.' He craned over the dashboard. 'This is supposed to be the place.'

Ariel gazed out into empty gloom. Nothing was there.

He tapped his phone.

No network.

'Although,' the driver rubbed his head, 'might not be the one I was thinking of.'

3

'Don't mind the cat.' The distracted grey presence fumbled under the counter for a form. He was probably only in his fifties but a lifetime of disappointment seemed to hang under his eyes and drip from the end of his words. 'Oh, for goodness' sake.' He swept the ginger tail from under his nose.

The Cliffs Hotel smelt faintly of lavender over dead cabbage. It called to Ariel's mind the elderly covering bad hygiene. An old transistor radio in a brown leather case crackled wistfully behind the counter, playing some chestnut of long ago. The receptionist turned to switch it off. Silence gripped the hall like a mildew.

'Will you be wanting a cooked breakfast?' he asked.

Through streaks of condensation on the glass, Ariel watched his taxi crawl down the long drive. One red fog lamp died away like an ember in the mist. He turned from the window with his phone in his hand. 'What I urgently need is some Wi-Fi.'

'I'm sorry?' the receptionist quizzed.

'An Internet connection.'

'Oh? You're the first person to ask.' He laid down his pen. 'I'm afraid management tends to avoid things that might detract from a break at the seaside, you see. Or actually, between us, anything that might be open to abuse. I personally don't see why – but in the end it's not up to me.'

'Is there ever a phone signal?'

'Patchy at the best of times, I'm led to understand. And in this fog – well. Though I did hear from one youngster that the higher rooms are better. Room sixteen, the attic room, might be best, if you point the thing out to sea.'

A stair creaked nearby. The receptionist stiffened.

'Then give me that room, yes?' Ariel made a lightning rod of one leg, jiggling to release stress into the floor. The rest of him was motionless save for a twitch on each cheek as his teeth ground inside.

Footsteps gave way to another man. He came bowling into the hall with the air of the house's master, patting down his last strands of hair. 'Ah! Our late arrival.' He was a curious man, pale and nervy, with a voice as hollow as an oboe. He looked Ariel over, lingering on his hood. 'We've stopped serving food, I'm afraid. But Rob might be able to rustle up some crisps?'

'Crisps?' quizzed Ariel.

'Potato chips.'

Laughter chimed up the hall behind the man. Ariel cocked an ear. 'You have a bar?'

'No, no,' said the man. 'Nuts if you prefer.'

'He's asked for sixteen,' said Rob. 'I could take him something up.'

'Nightmare.' The man found a registration card. 'And they were saying it isn't flying that's usually the problem in fog. Apparently most planes can take off and land perfectly well, and get about on their instruments – they just can't see to keep them apart on the ground. Nightmare, nightmare. Sixteen?'

'Excuse me?' Ariel was lost in a handwritten sign behind the counter that read: *You don't have to be crazy to work here, but it helps.* 'Please, if it has a signal.'

'Well, that's the thing.' The man looked up. 'Because we're in a bit of a dead spot. I can't guarantee how it'll work, especially today.'

'It's never been this bad, you see.' Rob leant around. 'Well, you'll know after the ordeal you've had. It's all over the news.'

'I guess it would be,' said Ariel. 'Flying from Boston to Amsterdam I didn't expect to end up on a beach vacation in the UK.'

'Oh yes, and it's a lot of passengers whose plans have changed, just like that. Even before you, they were diverting all day. I suppose the rest have filled the airport hotels, or gone down to London. We must be sort of a last resort,' he smiled ruefully.

'I beg your pardon,' sniffed the boss. 'We're certainly not a last resort, compared to some sterile airport hotel.'

Ariel shook his head. 'It's like travelling back in time.'

'Ironic too.' Rob pointed at the door. 'Holland's just over the way. A decent boat would've had you there in a few hours.'

'Then call it,' Ariel muttered. 'Please.'

'Well, you can't even see the road,' said the boss. 'So let's be sensible. Nobody's going anywhere tonight. If you want the room, we have it.'

'Sixteen, he wanted,' said Rob. 'For his phone.'

'Yes, I know he wanted sixteen.'

Ariel shook his head. 'I really can't spend the night disconnected, there are people waiting for me. Maybe I can use your phone?'

'Of course. If you give me a local number I'll connect you. For overseas calls you'll find the payphone beside the cloakrooms.' The boss flicked a gaze at Rob. 'We had the landline blocked after some guests abused the service.'

'Oh yes, there was an issue,' tutted Rob. 'The Canadians.'

'Then can you change some currency? I came direct from the plane. Or better – can you just call me a cab?'

'You won't get a cab out in this. It'd be breaking the law.'

'I just came in one. He's probably still on your road.'

'Well, I'm afraid there's a serious travel advisory in force.'

Laughter rolled up the hall as if in response. The boss frowned after it.

It was a zero-sum game. Ariel had two hours to get word to Zeva. The place seemed to be the only option for miles around. He reached into a pocket, pulled out a credit card and tossed it on to the counter.

'That won't be necessary.' The boss pushed it back.

'Really? Not even for identification?'

'All taken care of, sir. We were expecting you.'

Ariel nodded thanks, but resolved to be out by dawn at the latest. If need be he would walk to the nearest town; and he would do it tonight if the building threw up no signal.

'Show him upstairs, Rob.' The boss held out a key as big as a pizza slice. 'Room sixteen. The superior deluxe.'

Rob led the guest over a parquetry dining area. The smell subtly changed to stewed greens with a note of drainpipe. Moving to the stairs, Ariel took in the faded Constable prints, bad local seascapes, plastic ferns and feverish carpeting. Plus one old gilt-framed photograph of an imposing man with a moustache.

'Canadian, sir?' asked Rob. 'We had some Canadians once. Lovely people. He was actually in the Trudeau government and I think she kept horses. Or something. Anyway, government and horses I remember. Really nice folk.'

Ariel followed with his phone held out like a gun.

'Oh, I've done that backwards,' chuckled Rob. 'You said Boston. Usually you ask if someone's American and offend them because they're Canadian.'

Light faded behind them as they climbed, creaking, pinging, popping over carpeted floorboards. From the first landing Ariel glimpsed an adjacent wing through a window. In fog that Victorian pile glowed like the superstructure of a wreck, its angles cut into view by a spotlight somewhere behind it. Smudges suggested windows, gables and a portico under which a dim light shone. It was as if the place were built of smoke, as if fog had momentarily drifted into shape before wisping away to nothing.

Ariel pointed his phone around the landing, scanning for an umbilical link to anywhere but there.

There was none.

He was too disheartened to be irritated by the place. But these owner-operated places always irritated him. Unlike the lobby of a Hilton which belonged to nobody, these places made you an actor in some stranger's conceit of running a hotel. He had learnt across many childhood summers with his parents that the more charming a place, the more it was about the owner and not the guest. They were mirrors in which you couldn't see yourself. Plus there was something behind the knowing smiles, the quiet assumptions, that made the whole idea of your stay an in-joke.

As if sensing this, Rob gave a brief history of the Cliffs, punctuated with sighs and furtive hissing. The higher the pair climbed, the more his chat became an unburdening. It was uncomfortable. Ariel didn't usually attract unburdenings. But now he learnt that the Cliffs had once been a nursing home. He could have guessed it. Perhaps that old nature seeped through its skin, or perhaps the slow tock of the dining-room clock did its memorial work for it. After conversion into a hotel — mostly achieved by changing the sign on the portico — it had become known locally as the Spliffs, because bass and drum beats used to pelt over Bierstone

Inlet like skipping stones. In the village across the water, where folk slept in clothes against the cold, the music sounded like too much fun when fishing was bad, when little ones missed their dads, or when a boat hadn't checked in from a storm. Rob had started his job in those days, when the owners had believed in tambourines. But decadence had soon given way to control. The bang of it had come in the person of Clifford, the general manager downstairs, as uppity as a little dog. Between him, Madeleine the housekeeper and Rob, the duties of the house had become a chess game of subversions, every chore as stressful as burglary.

Apparently Clifford asked many things of Rob and Maddy; but the square root of them all was to isolate guests into two camps — one for those he thought the right kind of guest, and one for those he thought not.

By the next landing Rob hadn't the breath to continue. Whether from exertion or remorse for his indiscretions, his eyes pleaded out from his head.

Below him on the stairs Ariel was gripped by a fleeting déjà vu. He stopped and looked back. At the end of one summer, aged seventeen, he had stood at the top of similar guesthouse stairs and screamed 'I hate you!' at his parents.

The furthest frontier of childhood. The next day he acquired his first hoodie and never raised his voice again.

What Ariel Panek pined for now was a marble lobby and a burger. He wanted chrome, black leather, smoked glass, halogen spotlights, uniformed waiters, canned music. They were his chosen code. The lingua franca of acceptable humanity.

Because none of them could haunt him.

4

The attic corridor was narrow, its ceiling low. A security light flickering at the end of its life made the space seem to throb and constrict. Ariel checked the time. It was nine forty. Zeva's train would be approaching the Dutch border.

As he waited for Rob to open his room, there was shuffling on the landing below.

'Oh my God.' A young woman peered over the top stair. 'The Sheik of Araby.'

'Don't you disturb,' Rob pointed. 'He'll need his rest.' His tirade seemed forgotten as he held the door open for Ariel, softening his tone like a priest. 'Breakfast is from seven to nine, turn right at the

bottom of the stairs. There's tea and coffee on the
dresser. And mind, the towel rail gets hot. I'll nip
down for some biscuits and crisps.'

'Would there be a sandwich, by any chance? Or
even some cereal?'

'I'm afraid the kitchen's locked at nine. There
was an issue, you see. I don't know if there'll be
anything more in the bar.'

'So — there *is* a bar?' Ariel scanned the room
with his phone. No signal appeared.

'Well, I say bar — the residents' lounge. Except
it shuts at ten on weeknights.'

'Is that where the others are? I can hear some
activity.'

'There's a family party in.' Rob smiled patiently.
'I'll see they don't disturb you. Noise can travel in
this old place.'

'Don't climb all the way back just for me — I
can follow you down.'

'We stopped serving downstairs, you see. There
can be issues, after hours. You just rest up, sir. I'll
fetch all I can.'

Rob shuffled away. Ariel heard another set of
footsteps skip down the stairs before him. Then a
key clicked in a lock.

It must be the girl. From that glimpse she could be anywhere between twenty and thirty; which meant someone who wouldn't tolerate disconnection. Someone with a network, a screen, an idea. A signal. From first glance she'd seemed approachable, if strange. But the whole day was so strange that it made her a beacon of hope.

With connectivity Ariel would arrange his departure that night. In a limo, a boat, whatever would take him to a place with white lights and a connection to the world. There he would engage Zeva online, all night, thrill her till she hardly missed him.

He stood ordering his thoughts for a moment. The hotel in Amsterdam should be top of his calling list. Zeva would be unable to check in without him. If he called and left a credit-card number, they might even be able to send a car for her. With an explanation, with flowers. She could still be a princess for the night.

He looked around the room as if a signal might lurk in a corner.

The superior deluxe was a green room. It had a wicker chair and a dresser with a small television set and electric kettle. A double bed faced a bay window with a full-length mirror running down the far side. Unable to see a remote control, he switched on the TV at the set. The picture crackled up in black and white. He could only find the one channel, where some old movie showed a goose towing a dog through snow.

Ariel looked around again, as if relativity might brighten things. But the bed was too tall, an old person's bed with tucked-in sheets and blankets. If you fell out you would die but you couldn't fall out because the tucking exerted force enough to crush you to the width of your bones. A spider plant drooped from a pot on the windowsill. Its furthest leaves were burnt dead by a radiator below, which meant somebody rotated it so as to kill it evenly. The shower was a detachable hose in the bath.

Ariel lifted his bags off the bed, smoothing the bedspread. Nobody could say he had used the room. He wouldn't use the toilet or basin. He would leave without a word. Drop the key at reception and dispute the charges later. Wrenching up the sash window, he thrust his phone into the night. Chill tumbled in as he aimed it around, following clues from the hiss of the sea. But no signal came.

'Here we are,' Rob wheezed in with a tray. 'Found some pork scratchings and crisps. I'm afraid I couldn't find a nut for love nor money.'

'It's fine. A favour, though – can I beg some local coins for the payphone? I'll trade you dollars at a generous rate.'

'Oh.' Rob reached into a pocket bulging with keys. 'That won't be necessary. I'll see what I've got. Not much I'm afraid – oh, there's a pound. And forty, sixty – seventy.' He pressed the coins into Ariel's hand. 'That should do for Europe at least. Good night, sir. Let's hope conditions lift by morning.'

'Yes. Good night.' Ariel was touched. 'Do you feel things will lift by morning?'

Rob paused at the door. 'Well – this time the fog didn't so much come in as stay in. When the fog here is worse at midday than at dawn you know it's going to worsen more still – and it has. By teatime we couldn't see the village lights. So fingers crossed.'

'Yes, fingers crossed.' Ariel watched him step out. Then he huddled back at the window, listening to the creak of the stairs with one ear and the seething inlet with the other. Within a minute there came another rattle from the lower landing. A key in a lock.

Ariel pulled down the window and slipped into the hall.

The carpet's pattern seemed to writhe underfoot as he hurried towards the sounds. Footsteps pinged up the stairs when he reached the next landing down. Lighter steps than Rob's. He leant over the banister.

It was the young woman. Her hair bounced with each step and flew off her shoulders when she jumped the last stairs to the floor below. Ariel set off behind her. Three more flights down, the moan of a plank stopped her dead.

She looked up, giggling as he appeared in his hood.

She was slim and breezy. A tangle of ash-brown hair framed a broad open face, the kind usually pictured sprawling in meadows of flowers. She wore a filmy green dress and a cardigan wrapped loose like a shawl. 'Sorry.' She composed herself. 'I was expecting a top hat and tails. Not the Grim Reaper.'

Ariel smiled quizzically, slowing on the stairs.

'From the superior deluxe,' she explained.

'Ah. You mean my clothes? I didn't want to overdress for crisps.'

'I told Rob to bring you the last pork scratchings. Clifford will die. But he's got this salt-and-vinegar fetish, they're the only crisps he'll buy. According to him they go with the seaside. It's just so sixties, I detest them. I can tell you haven't tried one, I'd be able to smell it from here.'

'I didn't try one – after I saw the, uh, scratching?'

'They're what happens when you scratch pork,' she smiled.

Ariel gathered she had been drinking. 'So. I won't hold you, I just—'

'You're foreign.' She moved off down a corridor beside the darkened dining room. 'Hence the superior deluxe.'

'They said it had a phone signal.'

'A typical lie. My mother used to stay there. Today you can't even see the lighthouse, never mind use a phone.' She threw out her arms and twirled in a rapture, coming to rest under a light on the wall. 'But oh, the heated towel rail. Luxury.'

'Your mother?'

'*Mais oui.* She's in the lounge.'

'I hope I didn't steal her room.'

'She'll survive the Iconic Seascape Twin. I'll survive mine once I drown my little cousin. We're *en famille*, you see, and having to share.'

Her accent began to lose him. He straightened back to his mission. 'Well, I came out to find a signal. I have urgent calls to make.'

'Hopeless, isn't it? Though my uncle often gets one.'

'A signal? Inside the building?'

'Yes.' She wafted down the hall. 'In the lounge.'

5

Ariel followed the girl, watching her hair flash to blonde as she passed under lights. The pair passed a room that hummed with equipment, perhaps a kitchen. Its door was shut but Ariel turned his hood to it like an ear trumpet.

'Do you know which network your uncle picks up?'

'Come and ask him,' she smiled over a shoulder.

'Thanks, I won't interrupt. Just a few quick calls.'

'We're driving each other mad. Please.'

Tucked beyond the dining room stood a pair

of double doors. The smell of woodsmoke hung around them. Beyond, an older woman's voice, low and handsome, rang with authority. The girl threw the doors open on to a long salon.

'*Mein Gott!*' came the woman's voice. 'Olivia's pulled the young Chopin.'

The lounge was daubed in cosy light. A battered grand piano stood at one end, a fireplace tenderly crackled at the other. Lamps cast crowns and beams into a haze swirling lazily between them. Beside the fire an older woman in flowing gowns was moulded into an armchair, as if melted there with only her head and hands sticking out. By 'older' Ariel meant a woman whose lips were partly made of lipstick alone, and whose coif was streaked blonde, as lustrous as a wig. A woman one knew to call *madame*.

Gold flashed off her fingers. She flapped at Ariel like a child. 'I've always liked your polonaises. Don't we love the polonaises, Leonard?'

'I rather the preludes,' coughed a portly man at the other end.

Ariel shrugged. 'Sorry to disappoint you.'

'We're not disappointed yet, darling.' The woman cocked her head. 'Anyway, you look like you belong here. Doesn't he suit the room, Leonard, and the light?'

'My word! Renaissance man.'

A standing lamp shone gold on to the woman's skin, making a play between her and a gilded cherub on the mantelpiece behind. Ariel found the air thick with perfume as she met his hand, and pressed hers up to his lips. He had rarely kissed a woman's hand. The move was so candid that he bowed without thinking, even drew his feet together as if somewhere inside him lived a princely gene which she knew how to call.

'Margot,' she said.

'Ariel Panek,' he replied, and she splayed back to look him over.

'Don't panic, darling.'

Laughter burst out behind him. It was the same spluttering roar he had heard from reception. He turned and saw the gentleman shuddering with mirth, his mouth and lips glistening red. But instead of the briar pipe and tweeds that his round, balding form was built for, he sported striking casual clothes, almost a hippie's outfit of clogs, flared trousers and a billowing black and white shirt.

'For God's sake.' Olivia perched on a footstool. 'He will have heard that one.'

'Well, he will have heard it, darling, in his childhood,' said Margot. 'Which means amongst old friends — and that's how I want him to think of us.'

Keeping an eye on his screen, Ariel turned to shake Olivia's hand, greet her uncle Leonard and investigate a barrage of tiny tunes, beeps and booms that narrowed down to a boy on the floor behind a curtain. He didn't respond to the new arrival.

'The robot is Jack,' said Olivia. 'Just ignore him.'

No signal appeared on Ariel's phone; but they could take a minute or two to acquire. While he waited, he went to the bulging curtain and peeled it back. A chubby boy of about ten was there in a furry romper suit with animal ears on the hood. He didn't turn. Strange, Ariel mused, how times reflected human change. His parents spent their lives personifying their pets; now humans wore animal ears.

He cocked an ear to the game's noise: '*God of War?*' he ventured.

'*Neutron Rampage.*' The boy still didn't turn.

'Boom. I wrote the early code.'

'No way!' The child looked up. 'How do I get to gravitons?'

Ariel knelt over the game and flicked the controls. A starburst lit the boy's face. '*No way!*'

'Like Christ with the mutes,' chuckled Leonard. 'Bloody miracle.'

'You're a dark horse, aren't you, Panic?' Margot narrowed her gaze. 'Sweep in here with your smouldering eyes, your Viennese hoods – and now bloody gravitons to boot.'

Ariel kept his frown as he rose, letting a smile unfold after a moment. 'I'm a geek,' he shrugged. 'Gravitons rule.'

'God, that's so cool,' said Olivia. 'Geeks are so in. Are you stupidly rich?'

'Steady on, darling.'

'Sorry.' Ariel touched his phone to the window. 'Just a working geek. But please excuse me, I heard there might be a signal in here. If not I'll try the payphone.'

'Leonard, fix the man a drink.' Margot swept a hand through the haze, batting flocks of little vortices into the light. 'Tonight we're having Grand

Marnier cocktails. Or just Grand Marnier. Or cocktails.'

'Thank you, really – but I have urgent calls to make.' Ariel tapped his screen, shifting it here and there in the palm of his hand. 'This thing is so lost.'

'I often get a signal.' Leonard unwrapped a hand-kerchief and blew his nose. 'I've had one tonight. But the phone's upstairs with the little one. She goes mad otherwise.' With some effort he rocked himself to the edge of his chair and heaved on to his feet, steadying himself on an old gramophone that served as a table beside him. 'I've to check on her in a bit. I'll fetch it if you like, you're welcome to try it.'

'Seriously? It would really save my day.'

'A person could die of thirst,' called Margot.

'As in *you* could.' Leonard tottered to a window and pulled it up with a squeak, plucking liqueur and champagne from the ledge outside. He pulled ice cubes from a bowl beside them, blew off their frost, and mixed them into a tumbler. Olivia fetched everyone's glasses. When they were all shining full, Leonard closed the window and crashed back into his chair.

'Chin-chin,' he coughed.

'*Na zdrowie*.' Ariel raised his glass. 'It's that kind of day.'

'And what kind is that?' asked Margot.

'The kind where guests are more hospitable than hoteliers.'

'You've met Tweedledum and Tweedledee, then.'

'Jolly old pair, aren't they?' scoffed Leonard. 'Blind leading the blind.'

'That's a bit unfair.' Olivia stood off her stool. 'It can't be easy.'

Ariel's teeth began to grind. He resolved to find the payphone in the meantime of Leonard fetching the 'little one's' device. Leonard appeared to be in no hurry.

'Easy?' he said. 'Do you know, Panic, the best thing about the Cliffs Hotel is the sea crashing up the ramp so hard that it covers Rob's muttering. Inhale when the surf sucks out, curse when it bangs in, that's him. On days when spray whips up the steps he can swear whole bloody sentences.'

'Can he what,' said Margot.

'Most bitter man in creation,' Leonard went

on. 'Then in fog there's no surf, you see. In fog
he's as glassy as the briny.' He sipped his cocktail.
'Ah, the Cliffs Hotel: you can't even call it a cliff,
where it stands. Hardly a bluff. And you can't
really call it a hotel, in the usual sense. I'm sure
you had an earful when he took you upstairs.
Hmm?'

Ariel was prowling the room with his phone,
leaving no space unexplored. Only when
silence fell did he feel Leonard's gaze upon him.
'Excuse me?'

'I'm sure you'll have heard the Gospel according
to Rob. Hmm? Old Hardy Har Har, we call him.
Ever see that cartoon, with the depressive hyena?'

Ariel took a slug of drink, standing the glass
on a lamp table. 'A hotel should have Internet.
Especially when there's no phone signal. It's
ridiculous.'

Olivia smiled. 'I'm guessing you didn't come for
the view.'

'My flight was diverted to Stansted. This must
be the last room in the country.' He stared forlornly
at the phone. 'And you all? Vacations?'

'Memorial gathering,' sighed Margot. 'A sort of
remembrance.'

For a moment only the tinkle of ice and the popping of flame could be heard. When Ariel looked at Margot she was different. That moment held two views of her, like an old 3D postcard: hearty from one angle, suddenly fragile from another.

He made for the door. 'So. I didn't mean to interrupt. Payphone.'

'No, darling, don't leave us.' Margot reached out. 'Days like this are meant to be inclusive, to be celebrations. Aren't they, Leonard?'

'Benders,' Leonard snorted. 'God help us. Only way to deal with it.'

'Left, then left again.' Olivia pointed Ariel through the doors.

'I might have some coins.' Margot hoisted up her bag. 'Forty, fifty,' she rummaged, 'God, that's a shilling. Heaven knows what that one is.'

'Fifty pence between us,' laughed Olivia. 'We're so sad.'

'It's fine. Excuse me.' Ariel pulled the doors shut behind him. Muffled approval followed him up the hall: 'Well, well,' said Margot, 'lovely boy, dashing, sort of shy.'

'Splendid fellow,' coughed Leonard. 'Strange about the hood, but there you go.'

'Shhh,' hissed Olivia.

At least he was among good people, Ariel thought. And the drink had been welcome. He hurried around a corner, flicking up the number for his Amsterdam hotel.

The payphone was in the hall before the cloak-rooms. He poked in the pound coin and tapped the keypad. The line crackled and rang three times; then the coin clanked down as the number answered. He slumped with relief.

'The Excelsis Hotel Amsterdam—'

'Hello, listen, this is urgent—'

'—perfectly located within walking distance of Dam Square. Home to Chez Taekema, the Netherlands' premier culinary experience; or try Joostie, one of Europe's most celebrated watering holes, for a relaxed drink with friends. The Excelsis Amsterdam: an oasis of luxury in the heart of one of Europe's most vibrant capitals—'

Urgent beeps rang down the line. Ariel fed in the remaining coins, hearing them echo away like minutes of his life.

'—Five-star facilities with a personal touch, a conference centre for five hundred guests, and some of the best regional and international cuisine make the Excelsis your best choice for a uniquely tailored stay—'

6

A patch of haze in the lounge seemed to have trapped some golden light as it floated from fireplace to piano. The open salon doors pulled it over Ariel as he stood inside them. It descended spiralling around him like his last wisps of hope.

All avenues of independent action were spent.

His sharp eastern features sagged. He propped a neutral smile on his face as it dawned on him that relief could now only come through delicate, unpredictable circuits of rapport and generosity. Of humanity, and human intelligence.

Specifically Leonard's.

'Bottoms up!' beamed Leonard. 'Damnable

weather. We've been forced into a stupor, a sort of induced coma, while it all passes.'

'Not a coma, Leonard.' Margot ruffled through her robes and pulled out a lighter. 'We're as alive as being stranded in a cabin. It's an adventure. We must simply make a decision to admit we can't change it. A decision to enjoy it, like children around a campfire. Once we make a decision and speak it aloud, all the forces of circumstance can rally behind us. Isn't that the way, Panic?'

'Call me Ari.' Ariel found a chair near a window and fell into it.

'Sorry – Harry. And I'm sorry we've no more coins, money doesn't really change hands here. The little one might have some, Leonard, when you go up.'

'Yes, yes, must do that, and fetch down the phone.'

'Yes, darling, and tell her I'll be up at two.'

'You'd be doing me a big favour.' Ariel sat nodding. 'I can pay dollars, no problem.'

'No bloody way,' barked Leonard, 'wouldn't hear of it. It's yours. Anyway, I've that business going on in London overnight, I should be keeping tabs, not to mention on the little one herself.'

'Asthma, Harry. Poor thing.' Margot's lips gathered into pleats and concertinaed around a cigarette, leaving it blotchy with lipstick. Ariel watched her cheeks suck in behind her teeth, like a skull, as if molars had been removed to accent bone structure. 'But they won't be working in London now, Leonard – it's nearly one o'clock in the morning.' She blew a plume at the ceiling.

'For deals as big as this they're always at work,' said Leonard. 'One small remaining stratum of this country still functions, you know. It hasn't all gone to pot. I could hear at any moment. Any moment at all.'

'Well, I've never heard of the tax office working overnight.'

'It's not the tax office, it's a much more crucial agency between us and it. You can't just deal with the tax office point-blank, my God. Nothing would ever happen. You have to go above it and strike downwards. That's just what we've done.'

Olivia slipped off her stool and stretched her legs out on the carpet, lounging back with her drink in her lap. 'And who's "we"?'

'The consortium,' said Leonard. 'The steering body.'

Olivia rolled her eyes at Ariel. 'He's supposedly opening a museum.'

'Nothing supposed about it. Though I don't expect Olivia will be its greatest patron. She's at that age where she thinks we're barking mad.'

'I didn't say that. And twenty-eight is hardly an "age".'

'The thing is,' Margot waved her cigarette, 'it's such uncharted territory. Where's the night school with museum-opening classes? Where's the guide-book? That's why all the world's great legacies come from mavericks. People don't understand.'

'They just don't understand,' tutted Leonard.

'Anyway, Harry darling, won't you take off your coat? I think we're the only people in tonight, we should stick together. God knows there's not much to recommend the place otherwise. We're simply stuck. All in the same boat, aren't we, Leonard? Wouldn't even get the coastguard out.'

'God no. Hear that?' There came the groan of a horn in the distance. 'They're using foghorns tonight at sea. That should tell us something in this satellite-driven world.'

Ariel pushed back his hood. His hair was swept into its peak. 'They say the key to life is to change what you can and ignore what you can't. And I'm trying, believe me.'

He hated being a supplicant. Urgently needing something that others had the power to give, even offered to give, without actually giving it, left him in a beggar's place. Like a dog with only its eyes to appeal with, or a child left waiting in stupid shorts. He noted Leonard's reluctance to get the phone. Maybe the stairs were tricky. Maybe he couldn't disturb the child. However it was, being a favour Ariel had no right to begrudge him. But he felt a searing tension, boosted by visions of Zeva lost in a strange place, fretting alone in a lobby, or worse: meeting better company on some romantic foreign street.

Ariel drank. With each sip his hair seemed to hang straighter, his eyes sunk deeper under his brow, still twinkling out as his mind went to work on brighter things. If Leonard's device had a data signal he could rig a wireless hotspot and update his life at once: calls, text, mail, social pages in ten minutes flat. If the signal was insufficient he could try a call, or at worst a text, which would cost next to nothing. In any event, Zeva was now in Amsterdam on her own. The critical moment had passed and he would have to rely on her initiative until he could reach her. He watched Margot puff on her cigarette as all this ran through his head. 'You can smoke in here?' he asked when she looked over.

'Well, the fireplace is smoking more than I am.' She spat a cloud of blue. 'And why not? Unless, of course — if it offends you?'

'No, no. But do those guys live here, the managers? Won't they smell it?'

'Darling, who cares? I've been coming here for forty-three years — that pair of old blouses won't say a word to me. I've seen things here they will never see in their lives. I've played tambourine alongside Procol Harum. I've had pillow fights with Janis Joplin and the Mamas and the Papas *in this room.*'

'Serious? Wo.'

'Leonard's had piggybacks from Jimi Hendrix up and down the boat ramp, do you remember, Leonard?'

'Hrr-ha,' Leonard chuckled some phlegm. 'Didn't weigh quite so much then.'

'Well, you can only have been eight or nine.'

'Some family.' Ariel settled back, wrists hooked over the arms of his chair.

'This is just us, darling. The Borders. Take us as we come. What you see is what you get. Olivia's my daughter, a late surprise shall we say. And little Jack is my brother Leonard's, destined for great things.'

Olivia glanced at Ariel. '"Unlike Olivia" are the missing words in that sentence.'

'I didn't say that, darling. Be nice.'

Olivia held Ariel's gaze. 'And you're not obliged to say we look like sisters.'

'You could be sisters.'

'Thank you, darling. Wish I'd worn something slinkier. Though after all, you don't need to be very old to have a twenty-eight-year-old.'

'You don't need to be very young either.' Olivia hugged her knees to her chest, levelling a stare at Leonard as if through a gunsight. 'Are you going for this sodding phone then?'

'Eh?' Leonard coughed. 'Yes, yes. Give her ten minutes' rest, poor thing.'

'You've been going for the best part of an hour.'

'Yes, well, settle down, for God's sake.'

'Tell her I'll be up at three,' Margot said mistily. 'It's our remembrance day.'

'I hope I'm not interrupting,' said Ariel.

'Don't be silly,' flapped Margot. 'You're our guest of honour, isn't he, Leonard?'

'Good God, yes. We expected more faces, but, well – too fresh in their minds, I suppose. Terrible, this bloody coast is just voracious.'

'I'm sorry,' Ariel frowned. 'It's a death you're remembering.'

'My word, we are,' said Leonard. 'So the more the merrier on that front. The secrets this fog holds back – we're better off not knowing the half of them, aren't we, Marg?'

'Yes, well, let's not drag it all up tonight.' Margot wiped an eye with her little finger. 'The important thing is that we're here like old friends, doing the human business of remembering. We should be thankful.'

Ariel took in the crackle of the fire. 'After this I'll get some sleep. We'll only wake the hotel if I keep you up talking all night.'

'They're in a cottage out the back,' Olivia pointed. 'If you go to that furthest window, behind the piano, you can see when a light's on. Once the light goes off, they never come down. Regular as wind-up toys. Normally it's just Clifford, I'm not sure if Rob stayed back tonight or walked into the village.'

'You can walk into town? I should do that. Find a taxi, or a credit-card phone.'

'In Bierstone?' scoffed Margot. 'You'd be lucky to find a punch-up. And wait for daylight or you'll end up in the sea. Why don't you tell us a little about you?'

'I'm a mathematician. Computer science.'

'From somewhere east of Germany or thereabouts?' asked Leonard.

'Good ear. Poland. Now working around Boston.'

'Boston, mathematics, computing,' mused Margot. 'Machine intelligence work?'

Ariel's brow lifted. 'Yes.'

'Fascinating stuff. The singularity and all that. So exponential. But you know you won't crack it till quantum mechanics chips in.'

'You know about that?' Ariel sat up. 'You're something else. I didn't expect this conversation until the conference. Though as I say, I disagree with most anti-intelligence theories. Quantum is interesting but we don't know anything yet. It's a lot of answers without questions. I tried to introduce it into a thesis once – but something was missing, it didn't work in a practical sense.'

'The thing is, darling, humans don't process in a linear fashion. Doesn't matter how many processors you use, only quanta can entangle, atom to atom, and in a way which defeats the speed of light. That's what will hold the rest of you back.'

'Ah – but up to now nothing suggests that any intelligent process uses more than lightspeed. It's plenty enough in an object the size of a brain.'

'You're thinking very locally, my dear.' Margot used her glass to gesticulate. 'Under the many-worlds interpretation of quantum mechanics, the entanglement occurs between parallel dimensions. Universes acting simultaneously.'

Ariel's brow hovered up. 'Too far out for me,' he smiled. 'I haven't seen the evidence. You're right that many-worlds predicts infinite universes where everything that can happen does happen. And we've proven the entanglement of distant particles. But nobody knows much more than that. I personally need to see something in the classical world before I work on it. If I see one day that it might be true, I'll work on it for you. Okay? And meantime I name you Madame Geek.'

'Off to work then, darling,' Margot laughed. 'The answer's all around us.'

Ariel shook his head, grinning. 'It's like being stuck with colleagues.'

'Ah yes.' Leonard smiled up at the ceiling. 'The operative word being "stuck". Only one thing for it,' and he began rocking himself out of his chair with little grunts, ready to make for the window.

Ariel's face grew soft. His movements grew languid. He joined Olivia at the window as Leonard filled the drinks again, then carried one to Margot.

'Outrageous fortune.' She thrust the glass up.

'Outrageous,' toasted Leonard.

'It's our day,' said Margot. 'Don't you see? We're entangled.'

'I guess we are.' Ariel pulled out his phone and rested it in a hand. Now a red light flashed: the low-battery warning. He returned it to his pocket, making a note to charge it.

Leonard tottered back from the window watching the carpet underfoot as if it were treacherous paving. He sat at the piano, frowning at the keys.

'Are you married, Harry?' asked Margot.

'No. But my girlfriend's waiting in Amsterdam. At least I hope she still is.'

Margot caught his hand. 'Does she know you're here?'

'She's who I need to call. But I haven't had a signal since Boston.'

'Dear God.' Her face fell. 'The poor girl.' Her frown turned to a scowl. 'Leonard, go and get the phone. Some poor girl will think he's abandoned her! Oh, the poor thing.'

'What's that?' Leonard beamed across the piano.

'Will you fetch the bloody telephone! We've been waiting half the night!'

Leonard's beam collapsed. 'Now, Margot — she needs her rest, you've said so yourself. Poor little thing, I mean—'

'*Go!*' barked Margot.

'All right, all right.' He heaved himself up and wobbled out through the doors, muttering to himself.

'You big arse!' she shouted after him.

As Margot primed another cigarette, Ariel pondered how unequal human power was, that in a mass of any number of individuals one alone could be the fuse for them all. He had found the fuse in the room. It was a happy moment.

He began to word an apology to Zeva.

After a few minutes Leonard's voice cooed in the corridor. Gently, as if to a kitten. 'Darling — come on. There's a good girl.'

The salon doors slowly opened.

'Come on, poppet. Back to bed.'

A girl of at least seventeen took a step inside. She was translucently pale, skeletal under a T-shirt and sagging tights, with long tangled hair and sunken eyes. She clutched a phone, kneaded it till her knuckles glowed white.

'For God's sake,' Margot slumped.

Smoke hovered to the open doors in ectoplasmic blobs, rotating like specimens in a jar. The fire crackled no more.

'Now, now.' Leonard stopped in the hall.

The girl's teeth appeared. In one vicious swipe she tore off the phone's cover and ploughed its metal edges through the flesh under her forearm. Time slowed. She shook with tension, gouging ruffles like plasticine, curled layers of cream and blue-grey tissue. Ariel gagged. He could swear he glimpsed her bone in the gash.

Within a second, straight as a machine, the girl pelted both parts at the fireplace.

Ariel checked the others' faces. They were ashen and still.

Even the haze seemed to congeal.

After a moment Leonard sighed. He glanced around the party.

Then trudged like a chastened schoolboy to the fireplace for the phone.

7

A fly lurched from the shadows. It whined around Ariel as he walked the girl back from the cloakroom. Olivia went ahead to the salon doors.

Ariel twitched. It wasn't the season for flies. Plus the girl looked shocking – her colour shifted from duck-egg to grey as she passed under the hallway lights. Something was seriously wrong. She had taken pains to keep her injury out of sight, and had refused to have it bandaged, simply rinsing it in cold water.

'We should treat that some more,' he said. 'You don't have to worry, I know first aid. I was even the swim-team lifeguard back in college.'

He caught a glimpse of the wound. Petals of dry tissue, darkening at the edges. He could swear a vein was exposed, a grey rubber cord that swung as she spun the gash away. Yet there was no blood. Not even a blush of warm flesh.

'Harry?' Margot called from the lounge. 'Harry!'

The drinks must have gotten to him. Under his frown he calculated what he knew of the circulatory system from his first-aid training: she was dangerously thin, perhaps so starved that peripheral blood flow was diverted from all but her vital organs; or the wound could be old, perhaps so repeatedly opened that it had cauterised itself. Ariel glanced sideways at the girl. She seemed calm, even placid. As if nothing had happened, as if a gash had mysteriously burst through her skin. Only he seemed to remember the volcanic turn of minutes before, that lancing of some inner abscess, that coup on everyone's attention, or whatever it had been. His gaze rolled around the corridor, wary of any more shock. Because there come times in any life when classical laws seem to fray. Times when the impossible or unexpected forces one's mind to abandon its learnings and look for new patterns from scratch. And the beginnings of those times are the hardest. They pump shivers through the heart, turn lights up and down, throw echoes.

After scanning all the models that might explain his position, Ariel took refuge by thinking of daybreak. He could feel Zeva wandering Amsterdam as if her fingers traipsed over his skin. But daybreak was suddenly an alien thing, as occasional as Christmas, as rare as an eclipse. He couldn't shake a sense that familiar life was receding – Zeva, daybreak, Amsterdam, Wi-Fi – all growing distant and clouded. A beach might feel the same as it dried under the sludge of a thrashing tide.

All he really knew was that he had to get a message out; and then get out himself. Ironically, after all this the phone was in the salon. But whether it was broken or not, it was surely beyond use to him now.

With a rattle and a whirr the dining-room clock chimed three. A green eye curled his way through a seaweed of hair. 'You're Polish then?'

Ariel managed a brittle smile. 'You guessed?'

'Leonard said.' The girl lost her footing and stumbled.

Her ribs slotted neatly between his fingers and he pulled her back up. 'You should eat. Some fruit, some sugars. For strength. The body is hardware for the mind. If you don't give it power you'll also starve the software.'

'You're funny. I'm not a computer, you know.'

'We are kind of computers. What's your name?'

'Gretchen.'

He felt her breath on his neck. She craned over his shoulder as if to sniff him. Her scent was cool and damp, of slept-in laundry, of convalescence. She kept looking at him as Olivia opened the salon doors. Then, as he stretched across Gretchen to take a door, she leant in and pecked his cheek. Just so, as if stealing.

'What do you mean, "he's not available"!' Leonard stormed around the lounge with the phone to his ear. Ariel was relieved to find someone else on edge. 'The deal's within hours of completion,' Leonard barked. 'I expect all hands on deck. This isn't your common or garden launch, you know, it's something unique. It'll make all your names!'

The salon's magic was gone. The room was duller, the haze more acrid. The fire had given up waiting to be tended. Now it was a net of glowing ash.

Ariel and Olivia carefully sat the girl in an

armchair. She seemed as light as air. Margot trembled dramatically by the fireplace, smoke tangling around her hair. 'Leonard, for the love of Christ, will you just deal with the little one! I'll have a complete relapse – I can barely feel my feet as it is!' She turned to Ariel, wagging a finger at a footstool: 'Harry, be a darling – fetch me the stool, can you? I need to get my legs up.'

'I'll get it,' sighed Olivia, who was the closer.

'I'm mortified,' said Margot. 'If only Leonard had a decent rein on her. He's let her grow completely feral.'

Leonard stood clutching his chest, moisture sparkling off his head. There was a moment's quiet, some shuffling, his wheezing. Then he rounded on Margot from across the room, lunging at such a ferocious angle that he had to plant his hands on the piano to stay upright: 'Why does it always come down to me! You bloody raised her, you're the mother figure, you're the woman! If I knew what made any of you tick she might have turned out differently! But I bloody don't and she bloody didn't!'

'Look at the lines on my face, Leonard Border!' Margot roared. 'Look at the state of me, invalided through all your bloody carry-on. Barely fifty-eight and a cot case!'

'Fifty-eight?' he bellowed. 'Fifty-eight! You're bloody seventy if you're a day!'

'Oh, thank you, in front of our friends, Leonard. Thank you so much for devaluing me in front of everyone. I'm sure you'll be happy when I'm gone! And the way you're going about it you won't have to wait very long!'

'That's right, only think of yourself! What about me? You bloody twisted her, you let her get this way and I'm the poor sod who has to live with it day after day!'

'Shhh!' Olivia found a spot on the floor beside Gretchen's chair, settling and smoothing her dress over her knees. 'For God's sake.'

Ariel followed suit, sitting cross-legged at the other side of the girl's chair. As much as anything, he hoped to observe her, maybe see her wound and quell his unease. Not only his training but his nature told him that fear sprang from ignorance. Missing information created dissonance, he reminded himself.

Some crucial information was missing in this room.

Leonard stood heaving behind the piano. Margot took a quiet drag on her cigarette. She chewed the smoke, swallowed it, and after a pause opened her lower lip as one opens a boxful of butterflies. Smoke coiled out. She watched it rise and gently said: 'I'm not putting anything on anyone. It's the middle of the night, she's overtired, and it's your turn to have her in your room. Unless I'm very much mistaken, Leonard, unless I've laboured under some vast misapprehension, she's *your* can of worms. Aren't you, my sweet,' she wrinkled her nose at the girl, 'with your sad little arse?'

She turned back to her smoke.

'Worms is right,' muttered Leonard. 'Hurts to think what might have been if you'd had any maternal instinct at all. Didn't think I'd need a bloody dowsing rod to find it.'

'Maternal instincts are inspired in mothers, Leonard. And I'm not her mother. Olivia's been quite enough. And what of your paternal instinct? It's taken years to assemble a single coherent sentence out of Jack, so I don't see how *you* can talk.'

'I'm not her bloody father, am I!'

'Well, you decided to take her in!'

'Shhh!' Olivia scowled at them both.

Another pause, some breathing. A pop in the fireplace.

Then Gretchen stirred and sighed. 'Why argue?' she said flatly. 'You were both crap.'

The words froze in the air.

Ariel glanced from Leonard to Margot. The haze crackled between them.

Leonard's lips clamped shut. A squeak escaped under pressure. Finally he doubled over and exploded with the biggest laugh of the night, rocking with it, whimpering, choking on words.

Margot said them first: 'We were both crap!' she squealed.

'Ahh-ha ha ha ha!' Leonard collapsed over the piano. 'Ah-ha, ah-ha, ah-ha *ha ha ha!*'

Ariel sat up. He watched Olivia stifle a giggle.

Gretchen tapped her feet together, waving the empty tips of her tights like streamers.

The salon's tension lit like phosphorus and burnt in a flash, even left a smell. It was merriment so high and clean that Ariel was soon helpless himself, from simply watching the pair wrestle the breath to say, 'We were crap!'

'Dear God!' Leonard clutched his chest.

'I can't feel my legs at all.' Margot dragged a sleeve over her face, wiping away make-up and tears. Then she set off quaking again, and the sight of her gasping for words set Leonard off with her. Even Gretchen had to bite her lip. They recombusted, snorting, puffing, waiting for Margot to wrench out a punchline. The more they watched, the less she could say; the less she could say the more they howled. Eventually, doubled almost to her lap, gurning up like a quivering white frog, she found enough breath to squeak: 'Don't know which hurt more: the cut or the bloody comment!'

'Ah-ha, ah-ha, *aha ha ha!*'

Gretchen sat pursing her lips as Ariel and Olivia fell squirming to the floor either side of her chair. The pair saw each other uncontrolled for the first time, red, wet and contorted in ways that only terror, sex and laughter can provoke. It was an intimacy.

They breathed together, sang the 'ahh's and 'a-ha's that trail strong laughter. In between these Margot and Leonard tossed ropes to the girl.

'You know we love you, darling,' they soothed. 'It's not easy. We're sorry if we got some things wrong. Need a degree in psychiatry these days.'

In that salty, empty-gutted place on the way back from derangement, the kind that really does walk with tragedy, the kind meant by Freud – Ariel's unrest seemed to vanish into the smog. Suddenly all was well with the lounge and the world. He was fascinated. He had never seen such a gusting display of humanity, where polarities flipped, weaknesses reversed, unity was forged from collapse – and all without a trace of logic. The party had spun its own orbit from nothing, and against all the odds. Ariel always thought in terms of systems, sums, algorithms, it was natural given his work. But he knew he'd seen an extraordinary thing when the maths of it escaped him.

Now Margot and Leonard winced and clutched at their afflictions. It was an unconscious return to defaults, a resetting – she with her faulty legs, he with his chest, one then the other like antelopes snorting their rank.

After this Leonard limped round the piano and offered the phone to Ariel. The battery cover no longer fitted, and both halves were scuffed and blackened by smoke. But the screen was alight, and Leonard presented it like a prize.

'No, no,' Ariel waved it away. 'Come on.'

'After all this trouble!' cried Margot. 'For God's sake phone someone!'

'Here,' Leonard tapped the screen, 'at least scribble a text. Put in the number and we'll send it. Signal's up and down I'm afraid, but it'll send in due course. I'm sorry it's been such a bother. I had no idea it was urgent.'

Ariel took the phone. He added Zeva's number to a text and felt the stress dissolve in his veins. After a moment's thought, he wrote:

Check the news, you won't believe it. Flight grounded in UK, hotels full, stuck in a guesthouse without signal or wifi. Guest offered this phone, let me know you're okay on this number. I love you, today is crazy, see you in a few hours even if I have to swim.

'Come then, little one,' Leonard waved Gretchen up. 'Enough for one night.' He paused to wince. Margot answered with a sigh, then he limped to the door, pausing to beam back at Ariel: 'You must think we're barking.'

Ariel cocked his head. 'Barking — like dogs?'

'No, no — crazy. Barking mad.'

Ariel smiled. 'Don't joke. You spoiled my work for ten years. There's no way to program tonight into machines. The algorithm doesn't exist.'

Leonard stared and leant forward. 'Well, you're a damn fine guy. Bloody impressive, and it's an honour – isn't it an honour, Marg, such a "cool guy" on a dreary night like this? Who'd have ever thought it?'

'Harry? Oh my God, we'd be lost without him.'

Leonard yanked open the doors and walked out. The girl resumed her natural bearing, as vulnerable as a refugee, tights limp off the bones of her hips. She looked over a shoulder to smile at Ariel. As the doors closed behind them their voices faded off.

Margot flapped for a drink. Ariel fetched it and she brought it to her mouth with both hands. The mood fell away. If you were writing the mood's equation, Ariel mused, you would start with Margot's face. When it was up, the world was up.

But now her mouth sagged. 'I don't know what I did to deserve it all,' she sighed. 'Must've been a menace in a past life. But then,' she glanced at Olivia, 'she's only like this because there's someone new around. I've as good as been that girl's mother, and now look. I've never felt such shame.' She shifted her weight, wincing. 'It's the bloody father. Whole family was as mad as cheese, it's genetic.'

'All right, all right.' Olivia moved to the window.

'Another of Leonard's brilliant decisions. We told him at the time, but no.'

'Leonard sort of rescued her,' Olivia explained as she handed a drink to Ariel.

'You wouldn't believe it, Harry. Absolute murder for the poor girl, in that household. I'm not saying she didn't need rescuing. I just don't see why it had to be us.'

Ariel took the tumbler and went to his chair, lost in the space between moods. A downside of such spirit was never knowing when to press on or hold back.

Margot sipped her drink and gazed wistfully up. 'Ah, Harry. I feel I can talk to you. I feel you don't judge. You're a good soul. It's made such a difference having you around . . .' Her voice broke on the words. 'I suppose we're just stressed out. Aren't we, Livvy? Don't breathe a word, Harry, but everything I have is on the line for Leonard's project. Every last thing. And do you think he'll tell me what's going on?' She sucked noisily at her drink. 'He goes off on these fantasies and oh my God. If only you'd been around for him to talk to.'

The doors clicked open. Leonard puffed in. 'Please tell me there's a beverage.'

'Did she settle?' asked Margot.

'Settled all right. She's locked me out. If she doesn't come to her senses I might have to bunk with one of you tonight. We can sort her out in the morning.' He heaved up the window and emptied a bottle into his glass, tossing ice cubes from a distance and licking the spillage from his fingers. 'Bottoms up!'

'That bloody family,' muttered Margot.

'God, don't start.' Leonard took a slug, turning to Ariel. 'Main thing, though — your message was sent. There must be a signal in room twelve.'

'Wo, fantastic! I feel bad for all your trouble — but thank you so much.'

'Not at all, rather we feel bad.' Leonard went to his chair. Before resting his drink on the gramophone lid, he lifted it and fiddled inside.

Ariel saw him silhouetted against a lamp. His features were of a healthy child, intent, uncalculating, innocent. Ariel looked at Olivia as she settled on the floor. She flashed him a smirk and scrunched up her face, a salute between kids trapped with parents. He glanced at Margot, whose eyes shone like jelly from craters of green, searching up into a plume of smoke. Then a pop and a crackle filled the room.

Suddenly a guitar, soft and busy.

'Bit of Eagles never hurt anyone,' said Leonard.

'Jesus, you're trying to kill me.' Margot blinked away a tear.

Olivia was the first to close her eyes. She swayed and mouthed along, silently at first, then softly, sweetly singing.

Margot slumped back. By the time the song's chorus arrived her throat was taut with feeling. She sang harmony as Leonard went to the piano and began to accompany, gently racing along the keyboard, scaling heights, finally warbling up till his neck was veined.

The setting came alive. As if all their pressures found the same voice, a gale that blew through their tissue. Margot choked up. She flapped at Ariel and he went, felt her bones beneath her gowns, took her on his arm. Under the volume of gowns there was nothing of her, she seemed to float rather than walk beside him; and he curiously felt that he floated as well. They gathered at the piano where Olivia slipped beside him. He slid an arm around her waist and pulled her in, feeling her hair on his shoulder. When a curtain flew up and long-forgotten Jack fled the room with his hands over his ears, they laughed as one simple soul in the fog; and drank, sang and danced like children.

'Is this even orchestrated for piano?' Ariel marvelled between songs.

'He does it in his head,' said Margot. 'Runs in the family, look.' She nudged Olivia, and Leonard made space for her on the stool.

'The Masquerade Waltz.' He hoisted his nose like a maestro and the pair thundered along the keys, fingers dicing like pistons. Orchestral peals of music shook the air. Margot snatched Ariel to her chest, tears sparkling on her cheeks, and they whirled, trailing ribbons of light. Leonard flew off on dizzying tangents, dragging Olivia through rumbas, foxtrots and boogies before soaring back to the waltz.

On an empty stomach, in the presence of such spirit, Ariel's mind underwent a reversal. His pressures grew light and clear. Fears that earlier had stabbed him gave way to visions like scents after a storm. The airline would notify her if she called; mobile-phone signals could be patchy in the best of places; his flight's cancellation would be listed on the Internet; she would have seen the problem on the news; she herself could be delayed in Brussels, or stuck on a train without signal, even feeling the fault was hers. These were the probabilities. Being also a scientist she would understand.

Coincidences can simply mount up at random. It happens.

As for the conference tomorrow: he knew all there was to say about machines and human intelligence. He could sleep on arrival in the morning.

But this night, he had to concede, was way out of his hands.

Leonard finally rose from the piano. He took a drink and crashed down into his chair, sending it reeling on its casters.

Olivia toyed alone; the waltz rose again. Margot leant against the instrument, idly suckling her cigarette. She watched her daughter fix a gaze on Ariel.

'Typical result for you though, Livvy.' Margot winked at him. 'Either taken or gay.'

'Oh, stop it.' Olivia launched into a ruthless concerto, seeming to fill the salon with shattering panes. Ariel sipped the last of his drink and shook his head in wonder.

This was some family.

Olivia grinned as he watched. 'Do you play?'

'I wish. I love music. And it's mathematical. But in my family I'm the only one who doesn't play anything. I'm guessing your museum is for music, Leonard?'

'Eh?' Leonard turned. 'No, actually. Not at all.'

'God, Harry,' Margot laughed, 'don't be taken in by their party tricks. If Bright Eyes here had applied herself, after all the lessons we paid for, it might have come to something. They can't even read a note of bloody music. Either of them.'

Ariel's mouth fell open. 'Tell me you joke. It takes hours a day to reach anywhere near this level. I was convinced you were concert pianists.'

'You're sweet, thank you.' Olivia left the piano. 'But I haven't played a note in months. And I can't remember the last time Leonard sat down.' She smiled and there was something in her gaze, a knowing, a teasing that made Ariel an ingénue, he couldn't say to what. Again the laws of physics in the lounge were different than elsewhere. Aside from brilliance there was no answer.

He went back to his chair and sank into it. 'Uff. You all mess me up.'

'Grand Marnier does it to me,' said Margot. 'Need it intravenously while this museum business drags on. Between that and Little Miss Spinster here, still tied to the apron strings.'

The barb found Olivia. Her face fell. She swallowed a word and left the room.

Margot and Leonard seemed not to notice.

Leonard rode his chair forward with kicks and thrusts of his heels. 'Ah, yes. Not an easy business. Delayed another day I'd say, Marg. At least.'

With daybreak scarcely three hours away, Ariel rose and stretched. The ride was over. 'It was great to meet you,' he said. 'Thank you for tonight. Unbelievable.'

Leonard tottered over for a hug. 'Splendid fellow.' He drew back to beam and wag a finger. 'You take care — y'hear?'

'I can't get up, darling, my legs have completely gone — but won't we see you at breakfast? You'll need debriefing after all this.'

'Debriefing?' Ariel paused. 'But I guess my flight will leave early. We'll see how it goes. For now we'll just say *au revoir*.' He stepped to Margot's chair, folded her hand over his and kissed her most prominent knuckle.

She pressed his palm to her cheek. 'I do love you,' she sniffed. Then, lowering her voice: 'And darling, mind out for Olivia — she's terribly vulnerable just now, and you're such a catch. She'd hate me telling you, don't breathe a word. Promise me.'

'Ah!' Leonard exclaimed. 'Speaking of catch, I don't know if there's been a reply to your message. The thing's locked upstairs with the little one. As soon as I get into the room I'll let you know, leave a note or something.'

'Thank you.' Ariel made for the door. 'You're great hosts, you really saved my night. Anyway, your number will be on my girlfriend's phone. I'll thank you again from Amsterdam when I arrive.'

'Like *Escape from* bloody *Alcatraz*, isn't it, darling? But we're so happy you came. We wouldn't have wanted it any other way.'

Ariel excused himself with a wave and made his way to bed. He couldn't make out their conversation as he moved up the hall. But a conversation began in earnest tones.

He was happy to move on. Though he left the night with a nostalgia for surprising times, it was a roller coaster he didn't have to ride again to remember fondly. Beneath its rewards, the night's material truth also interested him. Perhaps because he'd acted out of character, stepped out of himself. The material truth was that he was a hotel guest, as were the family, with a room upstairs. He had stayed in much bigger hotels with more thriving lobby bars and never once been waylaid before. He could have gone to his room and never seen the family again. He ordinarily would have done so.

This time he hadn't.

Something in the material truth became invalid in the lounge. It was a bubble with its own truth. One he was vaguely aware of, without knowing the rules.

His mind drifted back to daybreak. He would set an alarm and snatch a couple of hours' sleep. The night's taxes weighed in as he reached the last landing: his legs grew heavy, their weight seemed to swing off the bone. His heart beat through his eyeballs, and his clothes warmed back the night's smells.

He tried to conjure images of a rainforest shower in a Hilton. But he couldn't. Even a marble lobby seemed an imaginary thing, from another life. Now a yellowing rubber hose beckoned from a bathtub in an attic. Relativity had settled in.

He slowed as he reached the last stair, squinting into the gloom of the corridor.

Then he flinched, and froze there.

Something crouched by his door.

8

The figure rose twisting upright like a spiral of smoke. It seemed to flutter in the shadows, as if moved by a breeze; but there was no breeze. If anything the attic trapped all the building's stale heat and was airless. Ariel stood silent on the stairs.

As his eyes adjusted to the gloom the form finally took shape.

'Gretchen?' he whispered. 'Wo, I thought you were a ghost.'

She wore a filmy nightgown, made lucent by the flickering safety light at the end of the hall. Ariel sagged. Such were the tricks of shadow and light. She rocked arching her back off the wall, toeing the carpet with one bare foot, as if stood too long at a bus stop.

'I'm bleeding.' She held out her arm.

Ariel wanted to say 'Finally', but instead approached without a word and took her hand. The corridor was too dark to see the wound. He opened his door and led her into the bathroom, flicking on the light. Her arm, not much wider than its bone, was streaked with blood. Puckered flesh around the gash made a crater for it, and every movement spilled some out.

'Ouch!' He grabbed a flannel and pressed it in. 'Does it hurt?'

She didn't answer but stared at him. Her big green eyes were as steady as a cat's.

'Maybe we should get Margot or Leonard,' he said.

'No!' she barked.

Ariel started. Her voice had dropped a tone, so harshly that it sounded like someone else. He paused, frowning into her eyes.

She quickly softened: 'No. There's no need to bother them. It doesn't hurt. It's just that you said you knew first aid.'

He carefully pulled back the flannel. The wound

didn't refill with blood, but he was glad that enough still coated it to cover his worst imaginings: veins and bones and all he thought he had glimpsed earlier. He caught himself thinking this, and realised he was taking pains not to probe the night too deeply any more. He was happy to accept easy explanations and leave them at that. It was unlike him. But he was somehow afraid of what he might find; and even that nagging sense he put down to fatigue from his journey, plus drinks and stress. He plucked a warm hand towel from the rail, wet it and rubbed it with soap before dabbing the gash, checking her face for signs of pain.

There were none. If anything, Gretchen's gaze softened even more as she watched him tend to her. Her lips, the fleshiest thing on her body, parted slightly.

'It's a serious injury,' he said. 'You should really have antiseptic, bandages, maybe even stitching by a doctor. You know?'

'It's okay,' she said. 'I've had worse.'

He dropped the bloodied cloths to the floor, took the last clean hand towel from the rail and carefully wrapped it around her arm. 'You'll have to hold it on. When you get to your room, tie it up with something, a stocking, or a couple of clean socks. Okay?'

As he turned her to the door, she leant into him. 'Can I stay? For a little while?'

He slumped like a marionette. 'I'm sorry. I have less than three hours to sleep, then a conference all day. I really need to rest now.'

Gretchen stared at her feet. 'A little while, though. Not long. I'm frightened.'

Ariel nodded wearily. Her little crush hadn't escaped him. He felt a certain duty to be gentle, and in that spirit guided her from the bathroom and said: 'It'll take me a few minutes to clean up. Why don't you wait for me? Then I can walk you to your room like a gentleman, and we can say good night.'

He fished a canvas amenities kit from his luggage.

'That's pretty.' She reached out with a bony finger, tracing the lines of a soaring red bird embroidered on the side.

'It's from the airline I flew with. The bird was on the tail of the plane, three storeys high. Do you like it?' He opened the pouch and showed the clutch of miniature toiletries.

'Oh yes,' she brought each one to her nose, 'they're like perfumes.'

'You can keep it if you like. A gift from me.' He was conscious of addressing her as a child; but it was all he could think to do – her fragility and innocence seemed to invite it.

Her face lit up as she clutched the gift to her chest. Behind her hollow features Ariel glimpsed her spirit, as keen as a puppy at an open gate. It touched and saddened him.

'I never went on a plane,' she said. 'You're awfully brave.'

'You don't have to be brave,' he laughed, stepping into the bathroom.

Ariel hadn't showered since leaving the States, but the bath hose could wait until morning. Leaning over the basin he caught sight of himself in the mirror. It made him pause. The light was strange; he looked even paler, more fatigued than he felt. Almost as white as Gretchen. Still, it had been a long day.

He washed his face and brushed his teeth, all the while thinking of her. From earlier snatches of conversation he'd gathered she wasn't family, but had been 'rescued' from a bad household. Apparently by Leonard. It had seemed at odds with social values at the time, a middle-aged man taking in a young girl. But that aside, it showed good heart. From first glance nobody could argue that she needed rescuing.

Ariel dried his face with the bath towel. Stepping out, he found the air laced with airline perfume. He drew a lungful, turning into the room – and stopped dead.

Gretchen stood naked but for a pair of tiny floral briefs. Her nightgown lay at her feet, the bloodied towel beside it. She was a barely uphol-stered skeleton, veined and pulsing, as luminous and gripping to behold as an articulated white worm rearing on its end. Her pants only touched her at the bones of her hips, sagging hammock-like between her legs. Tangles of ashen hair curled out, yellowing at the ends like a dead smoker's moustache.

She tossed her mane from her chest. A pair of nipples appeared, barely pimples in areolae that despite the yellow glow seemed blue.

'Love me,' she whimpered, reaching out.

Even as the words left her lips, Ariel's gape told her everything. He was a picture of revulsion and shock. She hurriedly covered her chest. Her face seemed to grow paler, wider, as if deflating. Suddenly her lips were separate creatures, slumping down at their ends. They trembled, and she ran hissing from the room.

'Gretchen!' He reached out to catch her. 'Hey!'

The air swirled behind her and she was gone. He listened out for footsteps but none came. As he reached the corridor, a door banged on the landing below. He twitched. There wasn't an inch of the corridor and stairs that didn't ping or creak underfoot; but she hadn't made a sound. Classical laws of physics and biology were frayed beyond comprehension. Short of someone having spiked his drinks, there was no explanation. He stood panting over whorls of mad carpet.

Stripped of his intelligence, the only remaining tools were simple human qualities: sympathy and hope. Whatever the girl suffered from, he hadn't meant to hurt her. He grabbed the nightgown from his room and tramped down the stairs. Room twelve, he remembered Leonard saying – but in the event he could hear her sobbing from the stairs. His sinking mood alloyed with seediness to make him feel faint.

'Gretchen?' He tapped the door. 'I'm sorry. It's fatigue. Come out and we can talk. I have your nightdress.' He waited, listening. No answer came.

Leonard's voice echoed up the stairs. Then Margot's. Ariel stiffened. He found himself wondering how Margot would make it up to bed. But as their voices drew closer he felt the gown in his hand. The material truth reared its head: he was a man in the small hours holding the nightdress of a girl sobbing behind a door in her underwear.

He quickly tried Gretchen's door. It was locked.

Leonard's voice drew near: 'Don't push it. We've all the time in the world.'

Ariel retreated up the stairs, drained and aching.

Guilt. A new ingredient. The night took on new shapes in his mind. It was a rotating apparatus, a wheel with hammers or a boom; or a pendulum that never passed through a centre but went from extreme to extreme — bang, take this, bang, take that. A quantum pendulum, living in two states at once, and as soon as you picked one it switched to the other. Opening his door he realised the night's tenor had been either high or low — but as soon as you realised which, the state switched.

Under all this, or because of it, ran a voltage, a substance whose media were adrenalin and bile. It was a fizz as sublimely sweet as pork fat, as ultrasonic as a dog whistle.

And always there buzzing.

An excitement; but also a fear.

This was the answer material truth couldn't provide. This was the bubble's oxygen: a fear, whose voltage once grabbed could not be let go.

He wondered if he was going mad.

The window in his room hadn't sealed. The air was comfortably chilled, and the TV still murmured, flickering in black and white. He switched it off, stashing the nightgown in a drawer beneath it, and kicking the bloodstained towel into the bathroom. With a teacup from beside the kettle he went to the sink and took gulp after gulp of water, so hungrily that it ran off his chin. Then he threw off his clothes, showered kneeling in the tub, and after squinting out to sea for signs of change, rifled through his bag for pyjamas.

Ariel knew it was all theatre, meant to claw back a sense of reality. But he had no problem with that. He believed in reality. He knew that it lurked most around ritual and routine. He felt that operating a human body was like minding a puppy; if you fed it one day at six, it would come sniffing the next day at six, and if you yawned it would lie down. In this way the taste of toothpaste and the ritual of pyjamas were his bridge to sleep — something never guaranteed with his flywheel of a mind, let alone on this night.

He squeezed under the bed sheets, kicking them up to loosen their grip. A breeze rattled the window and he clutched at the sound like a lifeline. Fog doesn't survive breezes. Daybreak approached, and there was a breeze. Surely the bubble had burst.

He fell into a tarry sleep, and a dream began with a feeling of extreme cold. He couldn't find the source of it. He seemed to churn like a plank in surf, unable to find up or down. Suddenly he was afloat with a view of the Cliffs Hotel ahead on a bluff. It pounced from the fog as the boiling whites of rollers thrashed around him. The sea was in the air, not delicately salted but dank with curdling seaweed, with worms and chains tossed up from the deep. Green peaks sat up foaming.

A swell crashed past him and he saw a body flash under its crest. He launched himself and grabbed its hand at the height of a break. Now they were two souls together, then he saw more floating in. They were all sucked back, pushed under, turned over in the surf, and his arms shot up to keep his bearings. When the swell threw him forward he rode it to the height of a boat ramp, scraping along concrete to a stop.

He looked up at the hotel, numb and exhausted.

Leonard was on the front step. 'It's not on!' he bellowed into the phone. 'If this is to go through we need all hands on deck. It'll make all your names!'

Ariel went to him. He snatched the phone just as a message arrived:

Woo hoo swishy hotel, ah ah do it to me baby yeah. Hey hope you landed ok, no problem at check-in here the Dutch seem really cool. Do I eat with like the conference or hide out or what? Hurry baby ah ah.

Then blackness. Not velvety as in literature but cool and oily, a gurgling away. A weakness not of babies but of the dead.

There was a knock at the door.

After a few moments came another. The rapping

seemed to slurp Ariel backwards into awareness, as if sucking him back through a straw. He stirred, glancing around, surprised to find himself in the hotel of the dream.

He held his breath and listened. A faint wheeze ran through the exposed heating pipes in the room, which to his groggy ears sounded like the distant chant of people, humans gathered somewhere in mournful song.

The knock came again.

'Ari? Are you awake?'

Ariel climbed out of bed. 'Olivia?' he called, fumbling for the door.

A ghostly shine like naked moonlight fell on him as it opened. Olivia stood hunched in a Chinese housecoat. Her hair was ragged and dull. No sooner had the door opened than her lips began to jitter and stretch.

'I'm sorry to wake you.' She fell into an ugly sob.

'Wo, hey.' Ariel pulled her into his arms. 'It's okay.'

Her weight pressed against him, and when he moved back, she moved with him. They were entangled, but such was relativity — her lithe, healthy mass compared to Gretchen's — that he held her all the more tightly, more sweetly, as if she were an antidote.

Still her sobs were so visceral that he leant out to check the corridor. 'Come in,' he whispered, writing off sleep in his mind. 'What's wrong?'

'There are things you need to know,' she wept. 'Don't be taken in by all the carry-on downstairs. It's so unfair, I can't bear to see you so lost.'

'Lost?' Ariel led her to the bed, sitting her beside him. She collapsed on to his shoulder, and as he stroked the hair off her face, his brain lit with adrenalin: it seemed there was a key to the night's algorithm. Something he would love to find out before he left. 'I'm only lost for a day,' he soothed. 'Don't take it too hard.'

'I don't know,' she snuffled. 'I don't even know where to start.'

'What do you mean? Is it about tonight?'

She shuddered, wiping herself on her gown. After a moment's quiet she seemed to rally, sitting up and straightening her clothes. She flicked him a rueful smile.

It was a lever. Ariel grabbed it. 'Want some pork scratching?'

'Stop it.' She swatted him limply, stifling a giggle.

He squeezed her, pulled her close; it was no betrayal, she was distraught. Clearly the family's issues ran deeper than he could see. Whatever it was, she could tell him now, in her own time. Come what may, dawn would soon break and he would be gone.

'Looks to me like you've had enough of the vacation,' he smiled.

'Oh God,' she sighed. 'Vacation? If only. We've nowhere to go. We're stuck with Leonard and his bloody project, it's just a farce, day after bloody day.'

'The museum? I'm sure he's doing his best.'

'There is no bloody museum. He ran a pub, that's all.'

'There is no museum?'

'He got himself in trouble with back taxes, and all he can think of to do instead of owning up is to claim that he's having the pub declared a museum and charitable trust so that it's tax-free. And then have it backdated. Like that's really going to happen. He doesn't even own the pub any more, he lives in a complete fantasy world.'

'So — a museum of beer?'

'The "Museum of Country Life", he says, on

the basis that a working pub is a living heritage installation.' She wiped an eye on his pyjama top. 'I feel so bloody stupid even saying it. It's insane. He actually phoned the tax office years ago and got some bloody forms that he carries around like royal charters. But half the time I even wonder if there's anyone on the end of his calls. He became obsessed with "making a mark on the world" and "leaving a legacy" – and it's just too late. Meanwhile poor Mum believes everything he says. He tells her every morning to be ready to leave at any moment, and she packs and gets all dressed up. It's just heartbreaking.'

'Wo. But maybe it's never too late? He's not that old.'

'Believe me,' she levelled a stare, 'it's too late.'

'So – you've been here a while then?'

She nodded, fiddling with his top button. 'I'm frightened to say how long. He's so fixated on clearing his name and making good. But the pub's gone. Everything's gone. I'm sorry to lay it all on you. You're the first balanced mind I've met in ages, and there are things you should know. This isn't the half of it.'

Her sobbing grew messy again. Ariel found

himself hugging and cradling her. 'Tsh, tsh,' he whispered, and her weight flowed into his lap, her face snuggled his belly, she traced its contours with her chin. 'You can tell me in your own time, tshh.' He adjusted himself, sat back to find pillows and prop her up. He was a carer now, she his charge. Intoxicating power for a man.

The damp of tears and salty breath are also sensual things.

Finally he parted her hair. Stroked it.

The tip of his little finger strayed on to her forehead. She pushed back on it, moved herself under it. He didn't move. It dangled there, a question mark.

Curling up with a sigh, her cheek drew beneath it. When she closed her eyes and snuggled up, it found her mouth.

She pecked the tip. He slid it between her lips. She suckled it up to the knuckle.

As he leant to her face, tasted her breath – there came a noise.

He stopped and listened.

It was a fly.

They jolted, spinning round.

Gretchen stood framed in the mirror.

ACT TWO

PART TWO

9

As thinly as Ariel's heart ticked when he woke, as grey as his skin looked in early light, all that mattered was that through the window he saw the sea pounding in, at least the nearest swells. Above them stretched a battleship sky, and in one unpainted corner – a patch of blue. Bright, with nothing between it and the sun. Gulls scudded and screamed.

He would soon be gone.

The room was empty. The girls had taken their teeming moods and left him to a fitful sleep. He would never know the secrets of the house and its occupants; and he didn't care. Because now the sun glanced off steel and glass, warmed the tarmac of roads and runways, forced all that it touched to yield to mathematics. It lit a world of classical laws and probabilities – his world. The only one he knew.

His pulse quickened.

It was after seven. The smell of toast wafted upstairs. The boss, Clifford, fussed around the dining room, perspiration gleaming on his brow. A radio played as Ariel stepped in: 'Sunshine after the rain,' chirped the announcer, 'and let's hope it's true or we'll want our money back! It's Elkie Brooks this Friday morning, followed by more top forty with Alessi, David Soul, Donna Summer . . .'

Alone behind huge sunglasses at a table by the mantelpiece sat Margot. It was the furthest table from the picture window, in the shaded half of the room, made darker by contrast with sunlight. She sat deadpan, as unmoving as a mannequin.

Ariel was surprised to see her so early – she'd barely slept as long as he had. Thinking about it, with the exception of staff, the whole place had roamed through the night. 'Good morning!' He made his way towards her.

'Ah! Dr Panek,' Clifford intercepted him. He

took his guest's elbow and ushered him to a table by the window. 'Room sixteen, superior deluxe – here we are.'

'Good morning, my darling,' waved Margot. 'We should have told them last night that you would take breakfast with the Borders. But it's more than anyone's life's worth to upset their little table plan. They're worse than bloody automatons.'

Clifford turned to glower. 'I'll thank you not to disturb the guests.'

Ariel looked around at the tables. His was distinguished by a fresh flower in a vase. He hung his bags on one of the chairs and turned to Clifford. 'Did my airline call, by any chance? I really have to get going.'

'Well, sir, I know your journey's important so I took the liberty of phoning for a car myself. Mr Malkin, in fact – the man who brought you. He knows the way, you see.' Clifford's offhanded manner of the night before had vanished.

'That's great, thank you.' Ariel couldn't account for the change towards him. Still, he was happy for it to remain another mystery of the Cliffs. Now he felt sunny and full of anticipation. Also ravenously hungry.

'And will you be enjoying the full breakfast?' Clifford smiled. 'Would you prefer white or brown toast? Tea or coffee? Eggs fried, poached or scrambled?'

'Brown, thank you. And fried eggs, with coffee.' As Clifford bustled away, Ariel went over to Margot. She was like an old queen, more propped up than sitting. 'Big night, eh?' He pecked her hand. 'Thank you so much, it was fun.'

Taking off her glasses, her eyes seemed deeper set, like raisins pushed in dough. She lowered her voice, leaning close: 'There's something going on down the hall. I've sent Leonard to have a look. You haven't seen Olivia about, have you?'

Ariel baulked. Sensations prickled through him, of Olivia's tongue, the taste of tears and skin. 'This morning? Can't say I have.'

'Dear boy!' Leonard rolled in just as a middle-aged woman appeared with a teacup. She must be Madeleine, whom Rob had spoken of yesterday. It already seemed so long ago. Madeleine evoked a scent of sweat, and sighed even before Leonard wagged a finger: 'Tell Clifford he'll be taking breakfast with the Borders. There can't be any problem with that. Just fetch his things over here.'

Madeleine shrank back. 'We've laid the table for room sixteen, that's all I'm saying.'

'Just bring the flower. Bring the flower and the cutlery. And the butter.' Leonard pulled out a chair for Ariel opposite Margot. He sat himself in between and huddled towards them, waiting for Madeleine to leave the room. Then he lowered his voice to a hiss: 'Bloody place is crawling with police.'

'What!' Margot stiffened. 'Whatever for?'

'The little one. Something's happened in the night. She's being interviewed in the sitting room behind the cloakrooms. I couldn't make much out.'

Ariel blanched and dropped his gaze.

'It can't be,' said Margot. 'She was with us half the night, then went straight to bed. I've been down half an hour and haven't seen a single policeman. Clifford hasn't said a word, neither Maddy – and they will have been here since six!'

'That's just them, isn't it. May as well ask the sodding cat.'

Guilt. Ariel grew filthy inside. If he imagined the events of the last hours as chess moves, he could see a game poised to turn badly against him. He thought back to the night: he'd insulted a fragile young girl in her first tentative steps towards flowering. He'd shattered any hope of self-esteem. Then she had watched him scorn her.

He was chilled to his bones. Unable to keep his face from twitching, he turned to look through the window. It was scaly, encrusted with salt. Outside beyond a gravel drive, the ground fell away to the sea. Mist was clearing. Blue soaked through the sky.

'I'm going to see for myself,' said Margot. She seemed to reverse from the table like an optical illusion, then swivel on her axis. It made Ariel's head spin for a moment, until he saw her emerge in a wheelchair. 'Harry darling, will you give me a push?'

The pair left Leonard tutting to himself and quietly rattled off to the cloakrooms. These led off a vestibule with a window on to the rear of the property, and two easy chairs with a coffee table between them, stacked with old magazines. Beyond ladies' and gents' lavatory doors, another door stood closed on what must be the furthest room in the building. Margot pointed it out for Ariel, motioning him to stop.

'Gretchen?' She leant towards it. 'Darling?'

There came a sound of voices, and of bustling and bristling, the kind that accompanies flak jackets bursting with pockets and pouches and tools. They clinked and creaked with menace, then a radio crackled.

Ariel's heart pounded. He was glad of the wheel-chair to lean on.

'Interview suspended at oh seven forty due to interruption,' came a gruff voice.

'Can I go now?' asked Gretchen.

'Sit tight for us, my love,' said the man. 'It's crucial that we get to the bottom of things while they're still fresh in your mind.'

An older female voice said: 'Shall I make a start on talking to the others?'

'Hold back for now, Constable,' said the man. 'We need to be clear about what we're dealing with. Also, I'd rather have a female presence at this interview.'

'Right you are, Inspector.'

The radio crackled again: 'Tango Charlie Three-Six: approaches secured. The area is sealed. Standing by, over.'

'Roger that, Three-Six,' replied the inspector. 'Headcount on the premises is three staff, four residents plus victim, and one foreign national, IC-one male. That's one person of interest so far.'

'That must be you, Harry.' Margot craned round. 'Whatever can it be about?'

Ariel reeled. He leant over the chair's handles, taking his weight off quivering legs. Fear alloyed with the stress of wanting to run for his life, towards a car that would carry him to a plane and far away out of there. It was all sealed with lovesickness for Zeva, an ache that grew in inverse proportion to his hopes of getting out. For a few exhilarating minutes that morning he had felt himself outside the bubble, thought that its cable was out of his hands. But now the voltage amped so high that he wondered if it could ever be let go. Now it controlled his muscles, and fried all his thoughts at their source.

The door opened an inch. 'Stay clear of this door,' barked the inspector. 'There's an interview in progress for Suffolk Constabulary. No one is to approach. And no one is to leave the premises until our enquiries are complete. Is that understood?'

Margot turned to Ariel as if for a prompt. He glanced back numbly. She cleared her throat: 'Yes, officer, of course. I assure you there must be some misunderstanding . . .'

'Are you the child's mother?'

'Well, no, although—'

'That bodes even worse then, doesn't it? If I were you I'd save anything you have to say for the formal interview. In the meantime, this door will remain closed under police jurisdiction. You'll appreciate that we cannot risk having witnesses influenced, even by a sense of others, who may be material to the case, loitering nearby. Is that clear?'

'Yes, officer, yes.' Margot flapped at Ariel to withdraw.

Ariel gazed trembling through the window. Sunshine travelled past in shafts under fast-moving clouds, as free as the universe itself. He realised that he had one opportunity to react according to his principles and not his fears. One opportunity to invoke the material truth, and perhaps be on his way. Although his voice wavered, and was higher-pitched than usual, he managed to blurt: 'Officer? I'm an international passenger in transit. I've only been here a few hours. My flight was grounded at Stansted and I really have to return.

I'm the speaker at a conference today in Amsterdam. I'm sure you'll understand — I must be on my way.'

The radio crackled and bleeped behind the door. Belts clinked, there came murmurs. Ariel even thought he heard a chuckle and a sigh. Then the inspector:

'Let me make this crystal clear: your position this morning is that of a person of interest to enquiries relating to possible criminal offences in the United Kingdom. The only option I will offer you is to be arrested now, and held in police cells pending completion of those enquiries. Otherwise you are to wait in the dining room until further notice. You are not to return to your room. You are not to leave the premises. I warn you this area has been sealed. If you set one foot outside this building you will be arrested and charged with leaving the scene of a crime. Do I make myself perfectly clear?'

'Yes, sir.' Each of the inspector's words was a stair; now Ariel lay bleeding at the foot of them. He turned and pushed Margot up the hall.

As they left he heard the female constable say: 'As soon as this is done I'll crack on with preserving the scene. Which were our rooms of interest?'

'Twelve and sixteen,' said the inspector. 'Take a swab kit.'

'Preposterous,' huffed Margot as they slid into the dining room. 'Whatever do they think they're playing at? And who on earth can have called them?'

Ariel didn't hear. He was dazed. He parked Margot at the table and sat beside her, eyes blank. His mind was upstairs in room sixteen – with Gretchen's nightgown and his towels, soaked in her blood and his DNA.

'Well?' Leonard leant into a huddle. 'See what I mean? Old Bill. The law. The fuzz, as youngsters seem to call them these days.'

'For God's sake, Leonard, keep your voice down.' Margot pulled a pamphlet from her bag and fanned herself. 'God only knows what she's told them.'

'Well don't get worked up, we've nothing to fear. Good heavens, where would she be without us? We've raised her like one of our own!'

'They seem to have an interest in Harry, of all people.'

'Never!' Leonard flew back in his chair. 'I'll not hear of it! He only saw her for five minutes with the rest of us! Didn't you, Harry? You weren't alone with her once!'

Ariel spread his hands like a mute. It was enough to propel their chatter away from him. He was glad. For the time being it didn't matter what they thought, because deep in his mind he began to calculate options for escape.

He'd thought of two possibilities by the time Clifford bustled in with a breakfast plate. Even in profile one could see the load of eggs, sausage, bacon, beans, mushroom and tomato. Madeleine followed as if on a leash, carrying a rack of toast.

'Over here, thank you,' called Leonard.

But the pair passed by like a choo-choo train, weaving between tables to Ariel's official spot by the window. They put down his breakfast, Clifford tweaked the setting just so, then he crossed the room again to catch Ariel's eye.

'Breakfast is served, Doctor.' He bowed and moved off.

'It'll make its own way over, will it?' bellowed Leonard. 'A homing breakfast?'

Ariel shrugged, excusing himself to his table. Clifford had done him a favour. He needed quiet to work out his position. He knew he had limited time to act; with each blow he lost the energy and spirit for more. He was dangerously tired, which added to rising stress and increased the risk of a wrong move. And under it all he struggled with pain over Zeva, with fear over what she must feel.

He finally began to sense the maths of his situation. The emerging model disturbed him. Because a bubble containing its own laws and outcomes was all very well – in a certain sense every family had one – as long as the outcomes stayed in the bubble. But with the arrival of police this morning, outcomes had leaked into the classical world and were at large.

He couldn't stop himself from glimpsing the night through a tabloid editor's eyes: disadvantaged young girl; hotel room; dead of night; gifts; nudity; blood; tears.

He shuddered and reached for coffee.

For now he saw only two options. The first was to gain access to Gretchen. Appeal to her, show his remorse, do anything hopefully short of making her dreams come true. The alternative was a more dangerous gamble: to simply hold firm and wait for her to slip up. Because whatever it was that she told police, in the end it would have to be false to convict him. For either plan, he also hoped he could count on Olivia's support.

This was as far as he got before Margot blew a kiss and wheeled herself out. Leonard tottered over to his table.

'Dear boy, dear boy.' He sat with a sigh. 'Not to worry, rissoles tonight if you're still about. Prunes and custard for afters. One of their better nights.'

Leonard began to systematically gather all the table's objects, line them up according to some invisible value, and redistribute them to exact symmetrical bearings across the cloth. He frowned, completely taken up with the task. Finally he sat back to survey his work, adjusting here and there.

'Do you mind?' He reached for a slice of toast and buttered it thickly, returning all the objects to their place. 'Anyway,' he said through a mouthful, 'on a brighter note, good news today. I think the eagle may have landed.'

Ariel looked up. 'The eagle?'

'The consortium.' Leonard stared enticingly. 'Things could be moving. In fact – well, you're a man of the arts, you'll know of Damien Hirst and Grayson Perry? We're trying to book them for the opening.'

'Hirst?' Ariel played along. 'I love Hirst. We're

almost in the same business, conceptual math. I want one of his sharks. Doesn't have to be large.'

'If they're on board we'll be made. Just imagine! Sky's the limit.'

Ariel nodded. 'So, but — what is it exactly?'

'A living gallery. A gallery of life. The timeless British public-house experience, mythologised the world over, now made fully interactive. Imagine: anyone in the world could interact with real locals in a proper pub. The wisdom of ages is there. Succour from loneliness. Relief from melancholy. No two days are alike — and that seminal resource could be global.' He slid into Ariel's face: 'And you know: it's not too late to climb aboard. Hmm? I've been very particular with the consortium for this, top drawer only — but I'm impressed enough with you to give you a shot. Even now, when there's no risk left to speak of.'

Ariel nodded slowly. 'I'm hardly the investor type. And today I'm trapped in a hotel trying to get to a conference. I could lose the job that would pay for the investment.'

'But a piece of this action — it could make your name! You can come in at any level, I'd make a personal dispensation.' Leonard sat ogling as if waiting to bite a juicy cake. He absorbed every nuance of Ariel's reaction, tongue lolling behind his lip. 'Hmm?' he nudged. 'And good God – a bit of fun. You know?'

Talking to Leonard was unsettling. Dinner, projects, investments. Behind all he said there seemed to lurk an acceptance that Ariel was there to stay. The more he thought about it, the others seemed that way too. He would put it down to oversensitivity if it weren't for one fact: so far they were right.

The place was becoming a kind of hell.

He nodded vacantly, about to steer the conversation towards Leonard's phone – he should redouble efforts to contact Zeva, even make a call, try to get news from her – when Clifford bustled over again:

'Here's your car I believe, Doctor. I can have a word with the driver, buy you a few more minutes to finish your breakfast?'

Ariel spun around. A taxi nosed into view through the window, the same car that had brought him. Sun gleamed off chrome barely three yards away.

His pulse raced; the way out was clear.

IO

The kebab joint near the station was cold, bright and stung with antiseptic. Tomatoes, lettuce and falafel lay under cling film in stainless-steel trays. They had the air of guests at the hostel Zeva had found for the night: a linoleum-and-low-energy-light-bulb experience with colours like infants' toys. She had fled that pop-art morgue by dawn, only glad of being able to store luggage there.

Warrens of rickety streets outside were busy crossing over from night to day. Shouts still rang out, but were gradually joined by the massed whirr of bicycles like flights of hornets. It was Friday morning in Amsterdam.

Zeva broke down when the first tram came by.

Trams to her were funereal things. Dense, rumbling, inexorable. Their carriages were coffin-shaped like hearses and the larger their windows, the more she could imagine catafalques, railings and top-hatted men inside. They were clearly built to have caskets laid out in them, end to end, and lit from above.

Trams were a bad sign. The trip was a bad joke. She would call her parents for a ticket home. She was on that rim of life where nothing mattered any more. She was stupid, cold and alone, and the kebabs looked bad.

But as she pulled out her phone, a light flashed. There was a message:

Check the news, you won't believe it. Flight grounded in UK, hotels full, stuck in a guesthouse without signal or wifi. Guest offered this phone, let me know you're okay on this number. I love you, today is crazy, see you in a few hours even if I have to swim.

Zeva felt hit by a dam-burst. An elation that made her blink up at the ceiling, as if suddenly learning that she never had to age. Tears pooled in the sockets of her eyes; she arched back to contain them, to bathe in them. Happy tears are hotter than sad tears. Her mind raced. On top of everything, the message reset her standing in the world. He was legitimately detained and must be on his way. He must be beside himself. She was no longer stupid. Now she could be sympathetic. She let out a quivering sigh.

The pair of Turks behind the counter sensed that she was in a parallel place. They stepped back. They had experience of stoners and of the mawkish drunk.

The algorithm of Zeva's morning spun to a new position, shining with dignity. She suddenly had credit for a certain amount of complaint against the delay, and against his frightening silence. Because only she had kept their pact of trust. When Ariel had said he would meet her, she had taken his words as an entire contract; she hadn't asked a flight number, hadn't asked a route. Even when he'd failed to show, she'd held back from phoning airlines, even from checking the news. If she took the time to calculate it the way her grandfather would've encouraged, she could leverage a position of power over Ariel.

Instead she blurted her answer right away, sent it like a cry from a cot:

I love you! Her tears spilled down the screen. *Hurry hurry do you know when you arrive? Let me know so I can go meet you!*

She wondered if she should call. If he had sent the message just now, he might still be there to take a call on the guest's phone.

But then – he hadn't chosen to call her.

She caressed the phone back into her bag. The Turks stood clear as she sniffled an order for the biggest kebab they could make.

Emotions, though, are an oceanic mass. Strong movement doesn't just coax new peaks but sets a whole reservoir sloshing, where crests are offset by troughs in as quick and profound a succession as the scale of the forces that moved them. So that within a minute Zeva regretted the kebab. More precisely, she regretted replying so quickly to the message; because she had spent a night in hell. In replying so happily she had in effect said, 'Kick me, I'm yours,' and it soured her.

A new message arrived with a ping as she watched the cling film come off the salads. She decided to savour it for a while; on the one hand so as not to appear too keen, and on the other to enjoy an interlude of hope and power. One of the cooks wrapped her roll as tight as a flesh wound. She gave him five euros, waved off the change, and stepped into the gritty morning light. Her breath rose in columns, and looking around she saw a chaparral of breath as people hurried to work.

She basked in it. For the first time since leaving home she was at ease. Her preppy clothes didn't matter. She was in an art film.

It wasn't long before the new message proved irresistible. Standing on a corner with a view of the station, she tapped her screen.

Around twelve. Meet me if you want.

Her face fell. *Only if I want?* she wrote.

Don't you speak English? came the reply. *It's simple you know.*

I'm sorry is that Ariel? Thanks for letting us use the phone if not.

The screen stayed blank after this exchange. The last message seemed brusque, whoever wrote it. If it was Ariel, it was a problem. She read and reread it, and within moments plunged back into yesterday's twilight, a nightmarish space where nothing conformed to expected laws. There was simply no heartbeat that a text message couldn't raise or squash in an instant, no hope it couldn't nurture or kill.

In the world of the instant, a text was the finger of God.

Perhaps that was why she spent her life stuck to a screen. Currents ran through it that made it a pacemaker with its own adrenal charge. That charge was an excitement; but also a fear. One whose voltage once grabbed could not be let go.

She watched the phone and took a bite of her kebab. It tasted bad. Dropping it into a bin, she strolled thoughtfully along a bigger street, out of the path of cycles and trams that seemed to fly at her from every direction at once.

Her screen stayed blank. The truth was that nothing outside of it interested her. Life between messages was a backdrop. She checked it under an auspicious-looking tree, and nothing came. She checked it on a busy corner. And finally at the centre of a large square behind a church, she checked it again, and there, as if the extra space allowed easier landings, one leapt to the screen.

Zeva lunged for it:

Okay sorry, now it's me. I gave the phone back. I love you and you and you!

Her heart leapt: *Jesus this is a roller coaster. I love you and you, just get here!*

On my way. And darling I will buy this number from the lovely Borders. That's my friends. I will buy it and write to you all the way so you don't get lonely.

Oblivious to the world, she tapped: *I love you my darling! And I love it when you call me darling, it's so elegant and mature. I'm standing in Europe watching pigeons and bicycles and being called darling! Weeee!*

That's so elegant and mature.

Ha! I hate you! Just get here!

Zeva sniped fallen leaves with her feet, skipped to touch branches. She stopped for a sweet pastry from a cart that blew vapour and it was the sweetest pastry she could ever remember tasting. When she checked her screen, true to his word, Ariel was still there:

Do you like my love darling? Do you like the things I do to you?

She cuddled the phone, grinning stupidly: *I love them all! I miss them and need them right now more than ever before.*

Which ones do you love?

The words took rein of her body as if whispered into her ear. She pursed her lips, peered secretively around, strolled coyly: *I love the way you touch me. I love your sensitive fingers, and your kiss. I love the sounds you make when we're close.*

And what other things? In bed.

Ha ha come on! Just get here and I'll show you!

A small dapper woman passed with a little dog on a leash. Zeva's smile was so broad that the woman smiled and nodded a greeting. Even the little dog looked up.

And the messages kept rolling in. The screen became a kind of heaven:

I want you to take a picture for me. Take a picture on your phone and send it.

Okay what, like of Amsterdam, where I'm standing?

A picture of you. A special one. A sexy one that will make me get there faster.

Hmm I'm standing in public! I can maybe do my face?

No it has to be special. I will tell you what to do.

Just hurry up! We can fool around all day! Weeeee!

If you love me you will do this.

Come on! I'm standing in the middle of town!

If you love me you will do it. And if you don't, there's no point me coming.

11

A gull battled gusts outside the window. By trying to hang in one place it did the work of a windsock, showing the force and direction of draughts shoving it this way and that. Like snores between these and the boom of the sea, Ariel's taxi burbled purposefully away. Ariel watched it gleam. All the little laws of physics, predictable and measurable, played around the taxi that material truth had sent to collect him.

The same material truth was that Ariel had a hotel room in a different country, where a sweetheart waited eagerly, where in a few hours he was to speak at the most important conference of his career. But that truth was outside the window.

The window was as impenetrable a barrier as an atom wall. Inside that atom, that quantum bubble, he sat in a seaside guesthouse embroiled in some wild and shifting theatre. He sat paralysed by fear and by his own classical logic.

His passport was in his bag. He could run for it. But the police were of the classical world, and the airport was a long enough drive that he would easily be apprehended before boarding his flight. What's more, he was guilty of nothing.

Leonard snapped him out of his trance: 'The little one has the phone, to answer your question. Can't say if you've a reply yet or not. It's her phone, in fact. She lets me use it, saves having to deal with Tweedledum and Tweedledee. I'll see if I can fetch it just now. As to our other business, think on it, old boy.' He slapped the table. 'The offer's open, but we'll have to move fast, events are gathering pace. And if you believe in destiny, ponder this: there must be a reason you were sent here. Hmm? Strange that within a day you've a chance to scoop the opportunity of a decade. Are you with me? Think about that. Destiny's a funny one.'

Ariel smiled bitterly. 'I don't see any police outside.'

'Believe me, the place is bloody crawling.'

Ariel leant to the glass, peering as far as he could down the track. 'But they obviously let the taxi through.'

'Perhaps, but just wait till he tries to get out.' Leonard spied a sausage shining on Ariel's plate. 'Do you mind?' He leant over and speared it, chewing half before rising from the table. 'I'll see if I can fetch the phone. Time marches on, and God knows she won't be using it just now.'

'Must be hard on her too,' said Ariel. 'She's been in there a while.'

'Gretchen?' Leonard scoffed. 'She'll be in her bloody element. Does nothing all day but watch crime shows. And with all the attention being paid her, well. Let's just say we shan't have to worry too much. She'll be lapping it up.'

Ariel's hand itched to grab his bags. As it was, after police orders not to leave the room, both Margot and Leonard sauntered around without a care. Olivia hadn't even come down, Jack neither. He looked around. All was quiet. He sensed that if any of the family saw him leave, they would innocuously report it if asked by police. Despite his innocence the move would indict him, and a hunt would be on. Moreover, fleeing the scene before questioning would get him locked up in itself. It wasn't that he thought the Borders suspicious of him in the least; simply that they seemed as artless and open as children. He wasn't sure of being able to conspire with them. Plus a compact of secrecy would incriminate them, which was too much to ask.

But now he was alone. Their simplicity of thought could as easily lead them to say he was floating around somewhere, just as they did.

His world outside the window was resplendent, breezy, and full of known laws.

Before he could think another thought, before his cumbersome logic could stop him, he snatched up his bags and hurried from the room; through the arch that led to reception, past the front desk towards the door — but there he stopped short.

'Bloody cheek if you ask me.' Leonard came fuming up the hall. 'They want you, Harry,' he said. 'Apparently you're to wait beside the cloakrooms until they call. I told them they're barking up the wrong tree — but I may as well have told the cat. As for the phone, well, I'd have more chance of tea at the bloody Kremlin.'

Ariel steadied himself on the reception desk. He waited a moment as Leonard huffed into the dining room and made a beeline for table sixteen. 'Finish my breakfast if you like,' he called after him, mostly for the comfort of his own voice.

'Do you mind?'

'No, go ahead.'

Then, with a glance at the world outside, he moved off to the cloakroom vestibule, settling in the furthest chair from the interview room. It was back to plan A: gain access to Gretchen. He sat wondering if the room had its own access from outside, or if not, how soon the police had been called after she'd run sobbing for the second time last night.

'Different day today,' came the female voice. 'Makes you wonder where it all went.'

'Yeah,' said the inspector. 'Hopefully France.'

The pair chuckled. Ariel didn't get the joke.

A moment later Leonard appeared, still chewing. He paused at the vestibule entrance, looked furtively around, then thrust himself forward from the waist. 'Harry,' he hissed, 'there's something you should know. I feel it's only right to confide in you.'

Ariel cocked an ear, frowning.

'Margot's in a bit of a bad way, I'm afraid. She holds up bravely, of course, but — well, she lived alone for a while, and we suspect that during that time she sort of gave up. On things, you know. Her divorce settlement was gone, and well — some of us in the family made a pact to lure her back out. And where I'm headed is — that's why we gave her a token involvement in the consortium. It made her feel responsible, needed, and she really does have rather fine taste in some things. But you should know that she has no financial involvement, and thus no directorial interest. She's embarrassed of her position, of course — who wouldn't be? — so I don't mind, and I warn you aforehand that she might rest her pride on it a little, and claim that she's all invested with us. I know you're a sensitive man. I'm sure I can trust you to play along.'

Ariel looked down for a while, nodding gravely. When he looked up, he held Leonard's gaze for a moment, and softly said: 'You know, Leonard — just then I was expecting you to say something important. I'm trapped here by police; my career, my relation-ships, my life are being broken piece by piece. And what you choose to tell me, like it was the answer to any of these urgent problems – is that I should pretend something for Margot.' He shook his head. 'Do the proportions of those two things – my situation, and what you just said – actually form any kind of relationship in your mind?'

Leonard nodded, blinking vigorously. 'Well, you say that – but you'd probably be surprised to know we've taken shares as low as five hundred dollars. Even lower, from the right people. Sum is no barrier. You just think about it, I shan't go on and on.'

Ariel's cheeks began to pucker rhythmically. He clenched and unclenched his fists. 'I really wonder about you, Leonard. I really wonder about you all, and about this place. Because while we're confiding things to each other, let me tell you something too: I am beginning to see this place as a kind of hell. Hmm? Does that seem proportionate?'

'Not a problem,' Leonard dismissed it with a wave, 'we have members from as far away as Asia. With me? It's all a question of the right people.'

'Stop that noise!' barked the inspector. 'Who's gathering out there? Shut up!'

Ariel detonated: 'I beg your pardon! There is an innocent man out here until proven guilty and you will address him with respect!'

'That's my boy!' Leonard beamed. 'Just what we're looking for.' He took a pantomime swipe at the door with his fist and wobbled away.

As Ariel sat shaking his head, the radio crackled behind the door: 'Yankee Victor, need support on the premises, a suspect's kicking off.'

'Roger that, armed response unit on its way.'

'He's not dangerous,' said Gretchen. 'Leave him, he's fine. I can talk to him if you like. He's really quite nice.'

'Hear that?' said the inspector. 'Completely under his power.'

Ariel heard the female officer sigh: 'The MO's report should be back shortly. Might get a better physical sense of what happened. Mightn't we, my love? Don't you worry, we'll look after you. Do you think you're okay to continue?'

'I'll try,' said Gretchen.

'Okay, that's fine. If at any time you'd like to stop, that's fine. Just let me know. We'll get some food in shortly. The doctor also said you should eat something. So let's go back to the beginning, shall we? The medical officer identified a wound on your body. Quite fresh. Is there anything you'd like to tell me about that?'

'Not really.'

'Okay, that's absolutely fine, my love, hunky-dory. Can you say if anyone here has acted badly towards you in the last twenty-four hours? Made you feel uncomfortable?'

'Here's a tissue, darling,' said the inspector.

Gretchen sniffled and blew her nose.

Ariel struggled through it with his head in his hands.

'That's fine, my love,' said the woman. 'A nice lady's coming to have a chat from Social Services. She'll be able to help with all sorts of things. And we'll get some food in shortly. Can you eat chips? Pies? Right old jolly time we'll have, while it's so cold out. Isn't it cold? Course, half your luck, wrapped up in blankets! You've beautiful hair, did you know that? You must be able to sit on it! I'd kill for hair like that.'

'Can we take a break now?' sniffed Gretchen.

'Course we can, as many as you like. Don't you worry, my love, you're safe as houses now. And when you feel well enough to tell us more, we can take the proper steps to make sure you'll be safe all the way down the line.'

Ariel heard some movement and sat back,

expecting the door to open. But it stayed shut. As he sat wishing Olivia would appear, he heard the ping of a phone receiving messages. The officers chatted between themselves.

'Bob, it is,' said the inspector. 'Down the how's-your-father talking to Pavel.'

'Crikey, that's twice,' said the constable. 'Or am I thinking of someone else?'

'May as well be. Barely got me head around the Poles, now it's Lithuanians.'

'Half of 'em is Russian is what I heard,' she said.

'Oh, bound to be. But I mean, they's all Poles in the end. Do you remember Frank's, down by the slip ramp? Polish shop now. You know old what's-his-name, where we had Judy's farewell? Polish shop. And the old butcher's.'

'Well, it's Europe, isn't it. I don't mind 'em. I'm not sure we got the best ones, that's all. My granddad in the war had Polish pilots on his squadron, couldn't say a bad word.'

'I don't mind 'em,' said the inspector. 'Except my Polish is awfully rusty.'

The pair chuckled darkly. Ariel felt filthier by the minute. But every word committed him more deeply to a waiting game. He would stick like a barnacle. Eventually either Gretchen or the police would have to deal with him.

In the meantime he sat making a list of all that didn't gel with the family and the Cliffs. All the slightly to grossly unexpected details, all the unanswered mysteries. And now the escalating horror. The list began with how he had even ended up there; for the life of him he couldn't recall arguing with airline staff at the airport over their choice of hotel, in fact couldn't recall dealing with airport staff at all. He'd ended up in an old taxi, had been driven blindly through fog to God knows where, and now was forced to listen to the equivalent of a radio play where a cast of officials he had never seen slowly incriminated him. He had no proof of their authority – for all he knew they were friends of Gretchen's playing the fool. Moreover, the only evidence that any police were outside came via hearsay from a man who lived in some fantasy world.

Ariel heard a door open inside the interview room.

'All right, Irene?' chirped the constable. 'Meet lovely Gretchen, our star helper.'

'Ooh!' Irene gasped. 'The hair!'

'I know! Scratch her eyes out!'

Ariel buried his head again. The room frothed over, cackling and cooing amid modest little sighs from Gretchen, until the inspector finally said: 'From a father's perspective, it bodes hair products. And hair products bodes hours locked out of the bathroom.'

Some more tittering, before Irene brought the full weight of Social Services authority to bear:

'Gretchen's a beautiful name. Don't hear names so nice any more, everyone's Ashley or Hayley or Britney. Course, I say that – one of mine's Hayley so I can hardly talk! So, my love, what I've been told is that there are some people in the hotel who are being held waiting until we see if something wrong has happened. Can you understand?'

'Yes,' sniffled Gretchen.

'Did something happen here that you'd like to tell me about? Has someone made you feel bad, in any way at all, in the past little while? We can talk about it when you're ready. You can understand we just need to know first of all if we might have an interest in any of the people in the hotel. By have an interest, I mean like ask some questions.

What I can tell you is that if something bad's happened to you — in any way at all — then we will protect you and make sure you don't have to face those people again. Do you understand? You can come away somewhere safe, and you won't have to fear anything more. So the quicker we know what we might be dealing with, the better things will turn out. If you believe that someone deserves to answer some questions then you'll be helping yourself by saying something now. But at the same time I want you to know that if it's too stressful we can wait till the end of the world. Is that clear, my love?'

A tiny whine escaped Gretchen's lips.

'Okay, I hear you. So it's a man? A boy? Someone in the hotel?'

Gretchen began to sob.

'Right. Well, you're very brave, and I say to you again — nothing will happen to you if you want to tell me more. Has he touched you, this person? Anywhere on your skin? Has he made you feel uncomfortable in any way? And Gretchen, I need you to be brave for me, darling, and take this the right way, it's no reflection whatsoever on you — but has this person seen you out of your clothes?'

Ariel slumped on to his lap. He kneaded his scalp with such force that the sound of it all but drowned out the interview.

Gretchen wept. 'I just wanted to be loved.'

'Okay, thank you. You're so brave. Could you show me what parts he saw or touched? Just point to them if it's private, to get an idea.'

There was a longer pause in the room. Some rustling.

'All right, my love, I get the picture. And are you willing to describe the person? You don't have to – and if all this is too much, we can stop. Okay? But it's not right, nobody has a right to do that. We'll stand behind you a hundred per cent.'

There came some clinking and rustling. A hushed word between officers. Then Irene: 'Do you need something, my love? Cuppa tea? Biscuit? Bit of sugar can do wonders in helping the body cope.' She paused for a dirty laugh. 'Or is that just me, as me hubby says after another stone's gone on.'

After an exchange under the officers' breaths, the inspector said: 'Nice phone. My youngest's got one just like it. You'd think it was surgically attached.'

'No, wait,' said the constable. 'She's showing us something on the screen.'

'Looks like a text message,' said the inspector.

'What's it say, my love?' Irene joined in. '*If you love me you will do this.*'

Ariel flew to his feet. 'Enough!' he yelled. 'I have seen no evidence of your authority! If you have an accusation then come out and make it but I will not sit here and listen to my incrimination through a door! Your procedures are wrong and suspicious! I have not been arrested! I am legally free to go! I am leaving to catch my flight and if you disagree then you can step out and stop me!'

He snatched his bags and stormed up the hall. A radio crackled behind him but the voices were silent. Somehow they must be a trick. All that was unexpected at the Cliffs had switched him to a watching mode, a passive mode from which he'd let fear get the better of him. All that was unexpected had disabled his capacity to judge, and to act.

Now he acted, carving through reception. He could see through the front door that his car had moved, or gone. He didn't care. He would march into town. By the time he flung open the door and slammed it behind him he couldn't believe how stupid he'd been. To sit through Gretchen's sniffling, to humour this madhouse, this hell. He knew no police would be waiting outside. He didn't even have to turn to know that none followed him. He flew off the steps and stormed on to the track, feeling the chill slap his face.

But looking ahead, his legs turned to liquid. He slowed, reeled, and dropped down his bags. His breathing grew laboured.

Lights flashed ahead along two hundred yards of track. He counted one, two, three police vehicles. Gathering speed towards him, barely fifty yards away, five officers were pulled by dogs jostling and rearing on leads.

And in the midst of this flashing swarm, like its queen, sat a fear he hadn't even got around to: a television news van.

12

Margot sat in her wheelchair against the wall beside the mantelpiece. Her sunglasses made her a sinister wasp. 'Here's the good-time gal,' she croaked.

Olivia paused in the doorway. Her arms were tightly folded. All of her seemed folded and withdrawn, and her hair was pulled back and tied with a ribbon. Her face was unpainted, pale and waxy with a yellowish tinge. When she took a breath and stepped inside, she saw Ariel hunched over his table by the window.

Only he and Margot were in the dining room.

She walked to within a table's distance of him and slowed, speaking purposefully. 'Thought you'd be long gone.' Her voice trembled slightly. She was like an actress, facing Ariel, still and unblinking – but seeming to address someone else, as if her speaking at all would pull a trigger. 'Don't tell me breakfast slowed you down?'

'Feel free to ignore me,' said Margot. 'I know you'd be happier if I was gone.'

Olivia turned. 'Oh, good morning. I just thought that by "good-time gal" you meant something other than "hello". I just thought perhaps it was a passive-aggressive way of pinning something on me.'

'You must really hate me.'

'I didn't say that.'

'Well, I don't know what I did to deserve all this. I honestly don't. Even Harry's turned against me. Don't bother denying last night, Harry. Jack's told me everything.'

Ariel slumped over his elbows like a trucker in a bar. 'Margot . . . I don't get it.' His voice was flat. 'I don't get anything any more.'

It wasn't an idle comment; having seen his classical world alive with police and cameras, the bubble was suddenly a refuge. As yet there had been no repercussions from his outburst, and he hadn't been back to the interview room to look for any. For now he followed the family's cues, and did nothing.

'Yes, well, blame it on me,' said Margot. 'Everyone else seems to.'

'Oh my God.' Olivia rolled her eyes. 'There aren't violins enough in the world.'

'You're not a mother. You just wouldn't know. After everything I've done. I know I'm not perfect. But I thought nobody's bloody perfect!' Her voice flew into a hysterical squeak at the end.

'Margot.' Ariel spread his hands. 'It was a long night.'

'I told you to take care with Olivia!'

'Oh thank you!' spat Olivia. 'What else did you tell him?'

'Isn't that bloody typical. I try to care for her, Harry, and she throws it in my face.'

'You try to care by telling strangers to watch out with me?'

'Ah! You see! I didn't say watch out — see how you twist every little thing? I said to take care of you! Look at yourself, Olivia, before you come pointing a finger at me!'

'You said take care *with* me. *With* me, Mother, which means *watch out*.'

Her tone hardened so much that Margot took it as a slap and bubbled with tears. After a moment she shrugged, seeming to surrender. 'I don't blame you, darling. Don't you see? It was Harry I was trying to rein in. I mean it's only natural, he's a red-blooded male. You're such a beautiful thing and so in your prime, and – well, a mother's concern, that's all. I wasn't blaming you, darling.'

'Excuse me?' said Ariel. 'Now I'm to blame again?' His gaze slid to the window. A patch of high-visibility vest flashed past.

'Oh, come on, Harry, I wasn't born yesterday. Jack said it sounded like lights-out at the bloody monkey house up those stairs.'

'Mother! We never even saw each other! I was long gone to bed! Hasn't it occurred to you, given that Gretchen's made another Armageddon of the day, that it must have been her? Scheming or chanting or whatever it bloody is that sets her off?'

The skin of Margot's neck fell in geological folds to her cardigan, pulsing as if weighing the odds by itself. 'Harry – is that true? I know you won't lie to me.'

'Of course. I slept alone. You know?'

'Oh, so you're saying I would lie!' Olivia rounded on her.

'Listen.' Ariel stood and led Olivia to Margot. 'Misunderstanding. Okay? Something worse is happening today.'

'But that's why I was niggled!' Margot flapped at Ariel to fetch Leonard's juice from across the table. Olivia was the closer and shoved it over, almost toppling it. 'That was the whole issue! You know what Gretchen's like, if she thought you two were cavorting it would set her off in a flash. She's at that difficult age.'

Olivia sighed. 'She's been at "that difficult age" as long as we've known her. You always think the worst of me.'

'Well if it's true, then, Harry, I owe you an apology.' Margot flapped for him again. 'Come, darling — I so missed you these last minutes. I was distraught. You must think we're barking, but we've just never seen anything like it, have we, Livvy?' As Ariel drew near she pulled him in and nuzzled him, knocking off her glasses and sending him under the table to fetch them. 'You're so good to me,' she croaked.

They joined the table. It was another giddy

reversal. Ariel felt a certain warmth; but one he disliked himself for. He was too broken down for much calculation, save to admit that whether inside or outside a bubble, it was better to have allies.

Margot rearranged herself, drew herself up. 'See? If we work as a team we can conquer the world. I'm just devastated when we fight.'

'But Mother—'

'Don't spoil it, darling. As it is we'll fight them on the beaches!' she laughed and shook both their hands across the table. 'Ahh, I'm so happy we're back together.' After some reflection she added: 'Rissoles tonight. But I wonder if we'll be splitting Gretchen's between us?'

'She doesn't eat anyway.' Olivia found Ariel's leg under the table and squeezed it. He eyed her sharply. 'And she won't be going anywhere, Mother, for reasons you well know.' She flashed Margot a warning.

'Mmm. Still, one can remember, and dream. Do you daydream, Harry?'

Ariel checked his watch. 'About my life ticking away, yes.'

'Ah yes.' Margot pulled out a cigarette. 'Atomic entanglement, eh?'

'Not entanglement. Machine intelligence. Though if I don't leave in the next hour I won't make the conference at all.'

'I didn't mean that.' Margot wagged a finger. 'I mean your entanglement with the life you think you're missing. Because although you're not there, it is going on without you, and you know it, and it knows it. You remain entangled. Mmm?'

Olivia's hand found Ariel again, stroking his thigh. He squeezed it before moving the hand off. 'I'm too tired for quantum, Margot. I'm supposed to be speaking in a few hours. Anyway, my first professor always said, "Throwing quantum mechanics into computation is like ending a novel by having pianos fall on all the characters."'

'Well, Harry, I hope you keep an open mind. There's more to heaven and earth than meets the eye — and for reference you should remember the key is quanta.'

'I love your certainty, Margot. Maybe you know something I don't. But in the meantime I'm afraid I don't share your ideas. The classical world is just fine for me.'

Throughout the conversation the rhythmic crash of the sea, the cry of gulls and the chime of the clock — it was ten — conspired to stir what little adrenalin he had left. It raised a fleeting eddy, and was gone. What gnawed at him now was a lower-frequency buzz that said he was growing used to his situation. Which said he had found a relatively comfortable niche in it. And which taunted him with this: that by simply removing his phone and connectivity for a single day, and leaving himself at large with no other tools among strangers — he had managed to destroy himself. It meant that in his usual life he used phones and connectivity as wormholes; escape chutes through time and space. If a situation grew too edgy in person, he would phone someone; if the call grew too dire, he would message someone else; if they became unrewarding, he would move to social media; and thus he never dealt with anything close or untoward for more than a second. Better still, this practice of wormholing via devices was upheld as a positive thing by everyone. Networking. It and the devices he helped invent had even changed basic pathways in the human brain. And these were upheld as positive too. As progress. And perhaps they were — as long as everyone concerned had a device.

And for as long as those devices had a signal.

For now his little hell involved nothing more challenging than the age-old algorithm of a household. A certain number of allies, a certain number of enemies, certain rewards to aim for, and certain punishments to avoid. He couldn't phone anyone wiser. He couldn't look it up on the Net. His only signal, faint as it had grown, was in himself.

And it was killing him.

Leonard's cough approached, peppered with exclamations. 'God only knows,' he huffed, sitting heavily. 'We'll have to see what she says. One thing, though: there's blood in room sixteen. Buggered if I know how that happened. She must have been in earlier. She does roam about. That must be it, she got in earlier before Harry went up.'

'Yes,' said Margot, 'it can only be that. Really though, Harry, if you're going to jet about you should lock your doors, in this day and age.'

Ariel faltered. 'I did. She came in the night. I tried to bandage her, that's all.'

'Hmm?' Leonard's brow shot up.

'Oh!' exclaimed Margot. 'So – she *was* in your room? In the night?'

'Godfathers!' Leonard clapped a hand to his

head. 'But you didn't get there yourself till nigh on four. What was she doing up so late? And why go to the attic? She doesn't even like it up there. It's all too strange.'

'I tried to bandage her. That was it, five minutes. Hence the blood.'

'But why didn't you say something straight away, Harry?' Margot cocked her head.

'I did. I mean – this is right away.'

'Well, it's not really, now is it? We've just been saying how she must have gone in earlier, then how you must have left your door unlocked.'

Olivia dropped her gaze. Leonard and Margot looked at each other.

'Hmm,' Leonard frowned. 'Not sure I like the idea of her being in your room in the middle of the night.'

'Leonard, it's not like that. I said I knew first aid when she hurt herself, and I guess she looked for me later when she started bleeding. You know?'

'Were you asleep?' asked Margot. 'Did she wake you, to bandage her?'

'Exactly. No big deal.'

'But I mean,' Leonard went on, 'it's not as if

she'd cut an artery. There's no reason for blood to appear on towels and bed sheets, fixtures and furnishings. Hmm?'

'Come on, it's not the St Valentine's Day Massacre up there. I used a couple of towels is all, and maybe she dropped a little here and there. I have witnesses that she didn't hang around, I mean . . .' Ariel shot a glance at Olivia.

She didn't look up.

'Well, it's just silly now,' said Margot. 'How could you have witnesses?'

'Starting to sound like a desperate man,' said Leonard.

Ariel fell quiet. Simple maths gave him two choices: to be a predator or a liar. No other course was open. Even if Olivia backed him up he was complicit in a lie with her, about not having met in the night. His mouth grew dry. Was he really a predator or a liar? Was he both, in reality? Because he felt like neither. And yet his position was firm. In the jumble of his mind he couldn't pinpoint where the tables had turned.

It confounded him. Scanning the events brought no answer, he felt he had acted nobly on each occasion: he was sympathetic to Gretchen when she was hurt; he was sympathetic to Olivia and gave reassurance; he was tolerant and kept his distance when Gretchen appeared in his room. And yet. And yet. Frustration surged through him, and he inwardly howled against the injustice.

'Don't see how you could have witnesses,' Margot sighed as if hearing Father Christmas exposed. 'Doesn't make sense.'

Ariel mustered all the clarity he could, leaning in to plead: 'Did somebody at least tell the police that she hurt herself? That it was nobody else?'

'There's a rum thing!' Leonard turned on him. 'Blame it all on her! We're all so barking mad we injure ourselves and report each other to the police, is that it? Show some bloody spine, man!'

'I can't take any more!' Margot collapsed over the arm of her chair.

'There, there.' Leonard yanked her upright, glaring at Ariel. 'We've shown you all the hospitality in the world. We didn't need the bloody telephone in the first place, but oh, no. Try and do the decent thing. We've tried to care for you like family, put you in touch with your loved ones, opened our lives to you, our hearts to you. For you to turn around and do *this*? Look at this woman. *Look at her!*'

'I only wanted to commemorate the fallen,' whined Margot. 'Is it too much to ask for an old woman, without all this having to happen?'

Ariel feared his heart would explode. Pressure leached away his sight, his ability to think. He physically shook with pain. Between shakes of his head, wild staring across the table and the room, he managed to say, 'Excuse me,' and escape to the hallway.

'Yes, walk away!' shouted Leonard. 'Bloody Polish bastard! You're no better than the gypsies in town! Walk away! I'm all right, Jack!'

He heard them tie up the matter behind him in squeaks and mutters: 'If he hadn't forced you to get the phone. Where are my Valium? Oh God.'

'I know, we paid full price for that good turn.'

'She was right as rain before he showed up. And now look. Where are they? Olivia, go and bring my little bag, the blue one. And see if you can spruce yourself up a bit – it's no wonder nobody wants you. Bloody hell, there's a predatory Pole on the loose and even he isn't keen!'

Reaching the quiet of the back corridor between

the lounge and the cloakrooms, Ariel heard a soft rustling. There, wrapped in a blanket with only her feet poking out, came Gretchen. Her tights sagged so low that she trailed the toes like butterfly nets, as her phone pinged away in her hand.

13

Zeva's pulse beat through her scalp.

Meet me at the airport. 12 o'clock British Airways from London. Message me when you're there and I'll give you instructions.

Yes yes my darling! she pinged back.

The central station swirled like a wintry pinball. At the far end of the concourse Zeva found the Schiphol airport trains. Her clothes didn't need smoothing but she smoothed them as if for the drinkers who shambled in football gear, and the grungy Van Dycks, Godots and Guevaras who shuffled around.

From the platform she glimpsed her train from

last night. It was bound for Paris via Brussels. She watched catering trolleys attend it, saw the driver climb aboard. How long ago yesterday seemed. Now the red and silver bullet train was part of her history. She wondered if some nucleus of angst and hope still hovered around her seat, was maybe entangled there for ever. She cast her gaze over the platform she had arrived on. Site of lost innocence. Before arriving, her imagination was of warmly lit stonework striped with shadows, where steam lapped at flower tubs having snaked across the wet. But in reality she had met with industrial concrete and strangers in hats. Still, it was only a practice run. Within hours Ariel and she would overlay new memories. The place was already an old stomping ground to her, etched deeper than most by the greater forces she suffered while stomping there.

Zeva's train quickly reached the airport. She rode an escalator up into a vast covered plaza surrounded by businesses. At one end, a gap was awash with packaged tulip bulbs and clogs, and a walk between them led to the terminals. Her arrivals gate, for European flights, was the closest. She examined the arrivals board but there was a problem. Flights arrived from three London airports; but none at midday. One arrived at 13:55, another at 14:05 and another at 15:10. It had just gone eleven. She looked around in case he was already there. But only drivers lingered at the back with names on cards.

Zeva pulled out the phone: *I'm here! No flight listed for midday tho, can you give me a number?*

A reply quickly followed: *Send me a picture and I'll tell you. I want the picture now.*

Hey! That's so weird, just tell me the flight!

It's not weird it's love. I want you to send me a picture of you naked. Right now.

You're such a dog. Don't freak me out, come on. Flight flight flight!

This is a test. If you don't send me the picture how can I know you love me? Go to a bathroom mirror if you have to and take the picture. Quickly or I won't come.

Feelings collided inside her. Elation met a sense that something was wrong. That a boundary was crossed. She scanned it against all she knew of Ariel, adding a tiring journey, a desolate night, perhaps some alcohol. But in the end everything rested on her faith. He might be messaging light-heartedly, recklessly, euphoric at being on his way.

The only problem was her screen; and as with all screens she just couldn't know.

Wow. You sure know how to keep the day moving, she replied. *Can't I promise something when you get here? I mean I'm right here in the flesh! Why settle for less!*

Do it. Remember my Polish side. I burn for this. I want to smell your skin off this picture. I want your face in it too.

Your Polish side is creeping me out. This isn't fair, come on. I'm so happy you're nearly here. Then you'll see everything! Smell my skin off my skin! Don't spoil it for me.

If you're saying that satisfying your lover spoils it for you then the flight is the least of your worries. Why should I come at all?

The message stabbed. She was unprepared to deal with it. Because unless he retracted it or revealed it as a joke – it showed darker issues than if he arrived or not.

A coffee bar sat a few yards away from the gate. Zeva ordered a flat white coffee and sat slowly stirring it on a table out front. She held the spoon upright and moved it round a clock face, mesmerising herself.

Inside her welled a raw charge, a stranglehold of frustration with an objective ache. It was amplified by her wanting to grant Ariel's wishes in principle, pretend they were fine for his sake; and by self-loathing for wanting to do it only to ease the pain, knowing they were wrong and unfair. She tapped at the phone, sniffling:

Are you honestly happy to let me feel this way? I'm scared.

No! Oh my darling I couldn't do anything to hurt you! I'm so desperate for you I just don't know what to do. My heart beats only for you, I just want to crawl inside you!

Date-rape roller coaster, she replied.

Please, please my baby. Please. Do you remember the film The Unbearable Lightness of Being? That's me. The doctor, all Eastern and hard, intense and passionate and dark like coffee. Please accept me and love me.

A smile popped to her lips. But it was jaded. She kept stirring her coffee, reading and rereading the messages. Her mind was abuzz with the maths of probability, something which in real life, with hard numbers, she was top of her class at. But in the world of limited text from a distance, and in the presence of fatigue, and shifts in the expected, she was lost. The question of how to feel about the chat fell on her good nature as a human. No intellectual clue existed, it was sinister and forgivable in equal measure.

Boy your Polish side is killing me. Hey but I love that movie too, we never talked about that. Except he has short hair.

I'll cut my hair. I'll do it for you.

Really? Woo-hoo, all change for Europe.

Will you swap it for the picture?

Stop! I'll think about it. Just hurry up!

I'm cutting it now. There's a hairdresser in the airport.

Now? For real? Hey well you send a picture too. But don't miss the flight! Which one is it? They have codes here for LCY, LHR and LGW.

LGW. I won't miss it my darling because I burn for you. I'm in a delirious fever, sweating in my veins and mouth and it smells of newborn wolves aching to suckle and kill and run for you howling your scent.

Zeva felt a spike of passion. The day's substance – an alloy of exhilaration, fear and anger – was within a percentile of the acids caused by obsession and dangerous love. Her heart touched that thrill. She had never spiked so high or fallen so low.

OMG you never wrote poetry to me, she tapped. *I love you! And that's the first flight arriving – yaaay! I can't wait.*

She watched the screen for six minutes more, rereading the last message, turning it round in her gut amid that voltage of stress. In some way the voltage detached her from the world like an electromagnetic field. A secret thing, it could exist alongside and within objectivity, but its laws were different. It made a space for itself inside her world, was a subset of it — but was not of its tissue.

It was eleven twenty. She wandered a circuit of the terminal plaza, drank a freshly squeezed orange juice and ate a pasta salad. Passing one shop, she spied a row of tiny teddy bears wearing jumpers that said 'ANIMAL' — and bought one to present to him, fondling it for a while with nervous fingertips, letting her feelings flow in before nestling it in her bag. The walk did her good. It was an outlet for nervous energy, and also a distraction; airports were resonant places to be, crackling with ions of change. Zeva made a point of strolling to the furthest arrivals gate before heading back to hers. Even from a distance she guessed it must be the long-haul gate — a different kind of crowd milled there, with a different feeling about them.

She daydreamed over the arrivals board, ran the exotic names over her tongue: Marrakech, Muscat, Paramaribo, Jakarta, Curaçao. With the nostalgia of a long-time expatriate she also lingered over home, New York, Los Angeles, and it was only then that she noticed something strange. In her trance she had missed seeing the piles of cut flowers along the gate's barrier; or perhaps her mind had filed them with the tulip bulbs in the plaza. However it was, her focus expanded, she blinked and gazed around.

Many of the flowers had notes attached. Beyond the crowd roamed TV cameras hoisted on shoulders, and lights blaring into faces.

Like hammer blows in quick succession, she saw that many of the faces were wet, and red; an instant later she spied a familiar news reporter from Boston.

The shock came to her as an image: nosing through icy skies over the last day or night, a plane hadn't made it home.

14

Gretchen's blanket slipped like a failing cocoon. She caught it round her waist, quickly hiding the phone in its folds. For an instant she peered up the corridor at Ariel; then she was gone without a sound.

'Gretchen!' he hissed.

There was no catching her. He moved back to the vestibule, strangely now a refuge in itself, a lobby of material truth. No sounds came from behind the door, and he noted his reluctance to open it; perhaps he couldn't face what he might find. Rather than take a chair, he climbed on to the broad windowsill and sat hugging his knees, side pressed to the glass. It was his bubble wall. He savoured its chill. Outside, the day grew dim. Fresh fog moved in – he could almost taste the slap of damp chalk.

Drifting into thought, he heard Gretchen find the others.

'Oh my God,' Margot trilled, 'come here, darling.'

'What is it?' called Leonard.

'The little one! Poor thing, you must be exhausted.'

'I am,' said Gretchen. 'And it's not over yet.'

'Oh?'

'Of course not. They haven't caught the perpetrator. They're surrounding the building in case someone makes a wrong move. Said I was lucky to be alive.'

'If I could hurt for you I would, my treasure. We've deduced what must've happened. You poor little thing. I've some Valium somewhere, you should take one for your nerves and have a nap. In my blue bag, darling. It's all too much to bear.'

'We're not to leave the building,' Gretchen went on. 'Whoever leaves the building will be arrested and charged on the spot.'

'Yes, yes, my love. It's all too horrid. And us happily going about our business. You just never know when you're well off. Leonard! *Leonard!*'

'Hmm?'

'We must call a general meeting – *Harry!* Olivia?'

'Haven't seen Jack all morning,' said Leonard.

'Playing his game,' said Olivia. 'Usual spot.'

'Ah, good lad. No need to disturb him.'

'Harry!' Margot cried. 'Oh for God's sake.'

'Shh!' hissed Olivia. 'Calm down. I'll get him, give me a minute.'

'Well, if he's gone out the police will have him!' Margot shouted.

Olivia's footfall left the dining room. Ariel heard it roving around.

A front of damp air preceded her to the vestibule. When she saw him she wrinkled her nose. Ariel didn't move. Her small black dress, her straightened hair flowing over pearls, the scent of her perfume, all belied the tenor of the day. 'God, I'm sorry,' she whispered, marching up till her belly pressed his side. 'Don't take it too badly.'

'Don't take it badly?' he hissed.

'Shhh.' She nestled into his torso. 'It'll blow over. Just hold steady.'

He spun round. 'I can't believe you! I'm blamed for an assault and you know the truth and let it happen! What's wrong with you? I could go to prison!'

'Hey, hey. If push comes to shove I'll be there, don't worry. Let them settle.'

'If push comes to shove?' He swung off the ledge. 'I've been trying to get out of here for a day! The last flight to my conference is gone, my career might go with it; the girl I was going to meet might go too. And some stranger who hates me is trying to get me locked up! I think push came to shove already, Olivia!'

Her gaze went to his mouth, and her fingers twitched to stroke him. But she held back. 'She doesn't hate you. She loves you.'

He exploded. 'Wo, really!'

'Hold it down or they'll come.'

'Some love!' he hissed.

'Aren't you the innocent one!' she giggled. 'As if it's your first day among people.'

'*People?* Use the term loosely.'

She tugged his collar, pulled herself in. Her lips drifted near his.

'Keep your cool,' she whispered. 'Let them have their say. We'll sort it out later.'

He strode back to the dining room like a fighting bull and made for the territory of his table. Gretchen untangled herself from Margot and hobbled to a chair, pulling it into a clearing and slumping as if on display. Olivia lingered as part of a loose circle that everyone but Ariel formed around her.

'Right,' said Margot. 'To start the meeting I think we should hear from Harry.'

He glowered from under his hood.

'Well?' She eyed him coldly. 'What have you to say?'

'Oh, is this a court now? Are you a judge?'

'Don't be so bloody flippant!' barked Leonard. 'Look at the poor child!'

Ariel took a deep breath. He studied the ceiling, counting under his breath. 'Okay. I'm really sorry that Gretchen is hurt – I'd like you to think back to when it happened. Maybe you remember that only I gave first aid. Only I did.'

'What are you saying, man! Are you accusing us of neglect?'

'There's just no reaching him.' Margot dabbed her eyes.

'No, no – I want you to remember that I cared, and acted immediately. To show my affection and concern and respect for you all.'

Gretchen fidgeted under her wrappings. 'The police want me in my room. Harry can go to his room but must stay in the hotel. Everyone else must stay down here.'

'There's a rum game!' Olivia tossed her head. 'I'm sorry but I'm going to my room if I want to, there's no crime scene in there.'

'No. You're to stay down here. The police said so. Code nine.'

'That'll be for forensics,' nodded Leonard. 'Did they say when we'd be free?'

'Soon,' she said gravely. 'You should all be grateful. I begged them not to bother us and they've gone on patrol outside until the results come back.'

'Results?' said Ariel. 'They didn't even speak to me, if I'm such a person of interest.' He stood and approached the girl. 'You know what happened – right? Why don't you tell everyone what really happened?'

'You're to go to your room and stay there,' she ordered. 'Or I'll fetch the police.'

He stood shaking his head at each of them in turn – then strode out.

Clifford accosted him at the foot of the stairs. 'Ah! Doctor. I take it you'll be with us another night?'

Ariel thought for a moment. 'Maybe. Maybe later I can use your phone and track down a higher authority.'

'Of course, sir, right you are.' And leaning to Ariel's ear: 'Under the circumstances, would you like some food sent up?'

'For sure. Thank you. And would you have a US-to-UK plug adaptor?'

'Mmm, not that I know of. I'll have a look just in case.'

Ariel went to his room and locked the door. He was tired now in the deepest sense. He had every reason to believe that police still swarmed outside. In a way he should be thankful that their barricade was far enough back to keep a media scrum off the doorstep. But it meant that escape, as far as he could gather from glimpses of the area, would have to be by sea. It was an idle thought because if discovered he would still be stopped at an airport, even in the Netherlands, once the alarm was raised.

Ariel's mind dealt best with systems, not chaos. As fascinated as he was with quantum mechanics, it was about unpredictability and chaos. It conformed to different rules, even made up its own as it went along. And although his stay at the Cliffs was more about chaos than structure, he refused to accept that a group of ordinary people with ordinary problems would not conform to ordinary rules.

So his mind went back to the beginning, he looked at his problem from scratch. The first step in any problem is to prioritise. In this case the broken system was himself. All parts except the hardware of the body were broken: his work life; his love life. Starved of the oxygen of communication. Maybe to their deaths, he couldn't know.

So which was more important? His love life. Because someone else was hurting. He must get word to Zeva. With Clifford's new demeanour he might find a way around the phone block. But he hesitated, not knowing who might answer the hotel phone if it became his point of contact. Police would also take an interest in that traffic.

He thought of contacting acquaintances at

London and Cambridge universities, asking them to relay a message to Zeva. But all the colleagues he knew would be in the Netherlands for the conference. Artificial intelligence was a small world at its sharp end.

After a while, something creaked on the stairs outside.

Rob was coming up the hall: 'No, mind. Come on now, please.'

And Gretchen: 'I can help. I'm not an imbecile.'

'I'm not saying that. Here, you knock on his door while I hold the tray.'

'Why don't you knock on the door and I'll hold the tray?'

'For goodness' sake. I don't want you disturbing the guest, do you hear? You're not to come up here. All right? Come on then – and careful, mind that drink.'

A gentle knock at the door. Ariel was already there. He opened it to find Rob with a newspaper in his hand. Gretchen held a tray of food and a glass of red wine. She had changed into a long silky dress, and her face was made up like a doll's.

'A little something to keep you going,' said Rob. 'And a paper, not that there'll be any good news in it.' Gretchen carefully inched to the dresser and put down the tray.

'Thank you,' said Ariel.

Rob swung behind Gretchen to push her out. 'Bon appétit,' he said. 'Come on, leave him to his meal.' They left and closed the door behind them. Rob's voice trailed off: 'Now don't disturb him. He's a proper guest. Do you hear?'

'It's not your hotel.'

'Well, it's not your hotel either.'

The meal was on an open plate. It steamed from the heat of gravy. A pair of large rissoles, which Ariel likened to meatballs, some mashed potato, broccoli and baby carrots came with a bowl of horseradish sauce, salt and pepper, a catering sachet of English mustard, a linen napkin and some heavy cutlery.

He sat on the bed and tore into it, stuffing half a rissole into his mouth and topping it up with mash and gravy. But after four mouthfuls he felt something break between his teeth. He slowed his chewing, straining food over his tongue – and isolated two objects.

They were tiny yellow pills. Similar to pills his mother used to take.

Poking through his mash he found another few.

Then came a gentle shuffling outside his door. He had moments to think.

There was no point resorting to accepted measures — raising an alarm, calling witnesses, as he might in the real world. The bubble's laws didn't work that way. He was on his own. As the door clicked open he lay back on the bed and closed his eyes.

He heard the spring in the door handle creak and pop, and the door quietly shut.

Then careful little steps.

Uneven breathing.

And the sound of scissor blades.

He sprang up and snatched her wrists. Gretchen gasped, dropping the scissors. They stared at each other, wide-eyed.

Then she swallowed a giggle.

He shook her. 'What pills are these?'

'Benzodiazepines,' she said. 'Valium.'

'What is this — a bad movie? Drugs and scissors? Is that who you are?'

She dropped her head, peering through the corner of an eye. 'It's a good movie. But you've got the wrong hair.'

He glared into her face, searching her eyes. She went limp and propped her weight against him. Despite his alarm it was saddening, her slight bony weight, like a gangling boy's. He was forced to handle her away, and finally to stand and hold her apart.

'Listen,' he hissed. 'You are wrong. I'm going to take this plate, these scissors with your fingerprints, and bring them to the police. You made the wrong move. Your game is over. Why did you set yourself up this way? For guaranteed failure? Is this who you really are? Is this who you want to be? For ever?'

'It's not failure,' she said softly. 'I'm here, aren't I? I just wanted to see you.'

'In a coma? With scissors?'

'Your hair's wrong. It needs to be like it was.'

Ariel shook his head as if shaking off a spider. 'Well, you know, Gretchen, I handled barbers for thirty years without anaesthetic.'

'But you mightn't want it. You mightn't know what the story is.'

'You drug people to do things they don't want? To get them into your "story"?'

'I'm Juliette Binoche,' she smiled. 'I'm your Tereza.'

'Then I'm SpongeBob. I'm going on to the street with this mash, these scissors, to show the police. If you don't care about me, I don't have to care about you.'

'But I do care.' She pulled a wrist free and gently moved a curl off his brow.

'So you have me trapped on suspicion of assault.'

'Well,' she shrugged. 'I might not be thin enough for you. You have to get to know me. I might not be pretty enough at first sight.'

'I'm getting to know you, for sure.' He grabbed the plate and tried to step past her.

'No!' She pushed him back. 'I'm in your room. All I have to do is scream.'

'You can't win,' he said. 'All the evidence is here.'

'If you leave I'll have time to write a note and jump from the window.'

'Wo.' He paused. 'You could teach game theory.'

As he said it he plotted the maths of their positions. It was twisted maths, not even a zero-sum game; because perversely, leaping from a window counted as a benefit to her. So that he, left behind, would lose more than the sum of her death in living consequences. In a game where he had a native stake, that is where he faced losses whether he invested or not – it was impossible to win against a party who benefited from losing.

'Here's the problem,' Ariel sighed. 'You're intelligent enough to know that you hold a bad position. That it's unfair. That it won't produce what you want. And if you know that, then doing it must also be hurting your dignity, which you don't want either. It's just loss upon loss. It doesn't add up. And listen carefully: if throwing yourself out of a window is a winning position for you – then you have to ask yourself who it is you're playing. If somebody in the past has hurt you, and you feel your death would hurt them back – then that is who you're playing in the game with the window. Not me. Hmm? If you're going to be a good gamer in life, you have to keep your games apart, remember that each different player is in a unique game. Beating one doesn't give you a win over any others. And if one beats you, that doesn't mean anyone else did.'

She turned away. As he tried to lure back her gaze, a tear splashed to her feet.

'Look at the form of this game,' he went on. 'The player is a person looking for love. She has three possibilities. One, to write notes and poetry and face an unpredictable outcome. Two, to do nothing and hope he notices her, and face an unpredictable outcome. Or three, to have the object of her feelings held by police, put drugs in his food, and attack him with scissors. For an absolute result in the negative.'

The images were so harsh that Ariel had to smile.

At this Gretchen smiled too, unwittingly. A beautiful smile under candid eyes. The moment was a connection. He pulled her into a hug. She rested her head on his shoulder and let her tears fall down his back.

'I just want to matter,' she whispered.

He stroked her, felt her vertebrae shudder with breath. 'Telling me that is more effective than drugs. You know? Now we met each other.' He pulled back to show his smile. 'The truth is cool. The truth is always elegant. It's disarming. It's all you need.'

She fell back to him, probing his arms with her fingers.

'Take a snapshot of right now. What you feel. Feel that? It's what you're looking for. It's what everyone's looking for. A connection. I mean, we can't have it in a romantic sense — but one human to another, this is the math of it. Remember it so you can recognise it again. You have a fine mind, Gretchen. It will do what you want. You're young and full of feelings. It can take you to a good place. A safe place. That's what it's for. But you have to steer it. You do! And it doesn't need police, or drugs, or scissors!'

She sighed and squeezed him hard. 'Anyway,' she said. 'I can still be your Tereza.'

'What do you mean?' he smiled.

Gretchen pulled back. Something stirred under her features, a new confidence blew across them like a breeze over a pond. After a moment, a subtle change came to her, rounding and softening her face. Her eyes flashed and locked on to his.

'I know you see other women, I know it!' came

a voice. It was sweet and heavily accented, but it wasn't hers, didn't even reflect the room's acoustics. It seemed to come with its own background from another place and time.

Ariel lost his breath.

'I can't bear this lightness, this freedom – I'm not strong enough,' she cried. A wild, sensual grin ran over her face, and she tossed her head back in silent laughter.

It was impossible. 'Do it again,' he whispered.

'Gretchen's a beautiful name.' It was the social worker – not an imitation but the voice itself. Gretchen beamed wickedly. 'Don't hear names so nice any more, everyone's Ashley or Hayley or Britney.'

Ariel couldn't feel his fingers. He gaped at her.

Her grin bobbed around before him, teasing, taunting. After a moment her eyes grew wide, and she barked: 'Headcount on the premises is three staff, four residents plus victim, and one foreign national, IC-one male.'

Then she took a deep breath, concentrating as if trying to force a burp. Her gaze narrowed, and the crackle of a radio burst through her lips: 'Tango

Charlie Three-Six: approaches secured. The area is sealed.' She doubled over, giggling.

Gears slipped and broke in Ariel's mind. In a fractured instant he wondered if the police outside were real. He wondered if anything was real, if he was real.

Gretchen gurgled like a baby, and after a moment's intense concentration rolled up her eyes and quietly said: 'Like I mean something to you.'

It was his mother.

The acoustics even captured his aunt Elena sighing in the background.

Gretchen had snatched a fragment of somewhere else.

He took his head in his hands. 'How?' was all he could mouth.

'They exist, don't they?' she laughed. 'Anyway, you're the bloody Einstein.' She lunged back into his arms. 'Kiss me and I'll tell them it was wrong. Kiss me and I'll tell them everything.'

Ariel reeled into the dresser. 'How many pills . . . ?'

'Kiss me, my darling.' She gripped his head.

He fell sprawling to the bed, newspaper crunching beneath his head. She began to swim before his eyes. Over his last delirious breath he heard the phone ping, felt her bones fumble over him. And suddenly came Zeva's urgent voice, as fresh as life:

'Where are you! Baby? There's been a crash!'

The room narrowed from the edges.

And vanished in a spin.

ACT THREE

15

A distinctive feeling comes from living on hope alone. It has a higher frequency than times even gently touched by probability. It's a kind of inflation, mathematical in that it must grow in inverse proportion to decreasing evidence. On a graph it can be described by an inverted U-curve: some hope is good, more is better, but too much levels the benefit then makes the curve plummet. It accounts for faces like those seen in critical-care waiting rooms. Wide nervous eyes. Fragile poise.

Zeva stood this way at the gate for the London flight. She didn't look in the direction of the long-haul gate. Of emotional necessity her focus shrank to what she needed to know. He was not on the flight from Boston, the one that appeared to be lost. He was coming from London, and his flight landed some time ago. She would soon see his face. She dialled his number again, but it rang and rang without answer or voicemail.

She convinced herself there was a queue at immigration. She knew he couldn't make calls from there, or from customs. And she didn't seriously expect that he would linger back waiting for a dirty picture of her. He was just held up.

The light was fading outside.

It would have been easy for him to let her know he had landed. In fact it would have been easy for him to be direct in all his messages. But then, he had travelled a long way, traumatically, and might not be himself. She was about to write a well-worded enquiry when a message pinged in:

Look at the form, it went. *The player is a person wanting love. She has three possibilities. One, to write poetry and have an unpredictable result. Two, to do nothing and have a worse unpredictable result. Or three, to deny him his deepest desires when he most needs them. For a definite result in the negative.*

Zeva studied the screen. For the first time the argument was built in a way Ariel would build it. One, two, three: *maybe, maybe, no.* It had a hint of game, which had come up between them more than once already, had even been applied to choosing sushi over pizza. She didn't like his argument, he was clearly still pressing for a picture – but she relaxed a little at finally seeing his influence, and with relaxation she grew weary.

You're intelligent and know it's a bad position, he went on. *Unfair. It won't bring what you want. And if you know it then doing it must also be hurting your dignity, which you don't want either. It doesn't add up.*

She thought for a moment before writing: *With my last energies all I can say is: if I added up every stubborn, selfish, controlling, unexpected part of you and separated it into one entity – then maybe I could begin to believe it would sound like this. Listen, no, Ariel – just come out. I'm finished now.*

Her eyes grew hot. Her ethic was changing. It was forced to in order to get what she wanted. Love was now in a race with dignity and pride, and they were neck and neck. Because, as the arrivals gate swirled around her, she didn't even know if he was there. She didn't know if it was him on the phone. But if it wasn't him, that didn't explain why he wasn't there.

She just didn't know. It was a vacuum.

And all the rules change in a vacuum.

The phone pinged again. She looked numbly.

I just really need you to do this right now. Can't you understand?

Zeva started walking again. She didn't reply. The only question in her mind: how much harder could things get? It was a game, a zero-sum; she could only lose everything she had inside, nothing more. But she was close enough to wonder how much that was.

The voltage spiked to new heights. She finally replied: *Why are you even writing? Thanks for this. An education. The plane landed hours ago. I'm scared to death.*

I love you! came the reply. *I wouldn't swap you for the world!*

She jabbed a response: *If you loved me you would have called me. It would take you one minute to explain. I don't know what happened with you.*

No! All right — send the picture and I'll call. Can't get fairer than that.

Acid tears scarred her cheeks. She stabbed at the screen. *Who is that really? You let me stand here all day, scared out of my wits. There are people crying out here, there are news cameras and I don't even want to look at what else. All you had to do was tell me what the hell was going on back there. I am leaving and if you want to catch me you can call and make a date.*

She switched off the phone before another message could arrive, and strode to the station. She knew the airport better than the neighbourhood she lived in. Perhaps this lack of novelty let her mind wander free, because now that the waiting was over, data began to run through her mind. Like a mainframe she crunched the numbers, sorted the patterns, and looked for a signature sum.

The longer messages, the later ones, shifted the maths. Riding the escalator to the platforms, she turned her mind to differences and omissions in the data.

During his year in the States Ariel had adopted the word 'wow'. He wrote it correctly but still thought it rhymed with 'low'. Thus he wandered the campus saying 'Wo'. By now so many students encouraged it that he thought it was an American institution. It was just an Ariel thing. The effect was that his world was filled with written 'wow's and spoken 'wo's. But none appeared in the messages.

There was another discrepancy: the word 'swap'.

She powered the phone back up, ignoring a pair of new messages, and scrolled through the day's history, skimming each text. There it was:

I wouldn't swap you for the world!

Ariel would say 'trade'. It was a concrete choice. An important one; because although communications had been out of character for him, tolerances had to be set high for screen messaging, you could never tell, nuances didn't show. It took concretes to judge beyond doubt. Lord knows they'd had enough spats over ambiguous texts, whether they were loaded, whether they were indifferent. Zeva knew that text conversations were minefields where the subtraction of an 'x' could change lifetimes.

But within normal tolerances, a falseness now showed itself. The messages had been too surprising, too up and down; and each time she had reacted they had become desperate and loving. They had a rhythm, a beat like a drum.

Her heart was the drum.

And now 'swap'.

She fired off a message: *Quickie: you win two cars in a lottery, what do you do?*

Swap one for a castle, came the reply. *Did you get a ticket?*

No but I'll make a deal with you. Send me your picture and I'll send you a really hot one, the bathrooms are empty right now.

A message flew back. She opened it to find a head shot of Ariel with his eyes closed, smiling distantly. He appeared to have newsprint behind him. It was taken in darkness, fuzzy and yellow, black at the corners. But he was there. Somewhere. With short hair off his ears. Scrolling down she saw the text: *Now who's not fair?*

She magnified the picture. Clumps of hair lay on the paper behind his head. Nobody cuts their hair lying down. Bringing the screen to her eye, she shivered.

He was unconscious.

Her heart thumped. The only link she had with Ariel was this number on her phone. She had to find him, or alert police. But she couldn't even say if any of the messages were his. The first seemed the most genuine, and had mentioned a guesthouse in the UK. A later message named the Borders as his friends.

However things were, she knew the number was connected to him, he was beside it, because the picture had come within seconds of asking for it. She stood breathless, calculating the options. There had been certain long gaps between messages. She wondered if the phone changed hands during those times, if there was a chance of reaching someone else, and getting an address, or raising an alarm.

She had to keep phoning the number. It had to ring and ring until the messager grew tired or someone else picked it up. Or better: she would keep the game going.

She fired off another message: *I'm in the bathroom, wanna play zipcode lottery to see how much I take off? Start with a digit from where you were.*

Ha ha you're trying to get an address, came the reply.

Zeva thought for a moment. *What do you mean? I'm trying to make the thing fun!*

Well if I'm supposed to be in the airport it makes you

pretty stupid because we have the same postcode. And we wouldn't even know what it is.

Zeva wandered in a trance, thinking hard. There seemed to be no way past the messager. She thought and thought, even drawing on logic from Ariel's lectures, stripping the issue to its basics. The insurmountable problem was now a person. She didn't know who the person was. She couldn't know. The two parties were her, whom she knew – and someone else, whom she didn't. They communicated with each other by messaging. Via mobile phones. Via technology.

Technology. An idea took root. Having thought of Ariel and his lectures, her mind flew back to her everyday life. To the hundreds of graduates, undergraduates and professors, the geeks and nerds and geniuses she mixed with every day. She narrowed them down to the crew from the Comms lab.

Her battery was running low, but she flicked through her contacts and hit a number back home. It answered after two rings.

'Brady? Zeva – listen, real quick: if I gave you a random foreign cellphone number would you be able to ping it?'

'If it's switched on. Someone lose their phone or what?'

'I'll tell you later, this is real urgent and my battery's dying. Will you be able to boil it down to like a map coordinate? Or a zipcode, even better?'

'How foreign are we talking?'

'I think United Kingdom.'

'Is the number local to there? Is it stationary? And are we talking metro area?'

'Yeah, I guess it's local, stationary, and I think out of town.' Zeva tapped her feet, swaying from side to side.

'Yeah, I can triangulate a position from the comms towers it uses. But I have to connect to the number. Means you owe me a beer.'

Zeva read the number off her screen, agreeing to save battery power until he called back in thirty minutes. She promised a case of beer, and hugged the phone to her chest. Technology is the way, the truth and the life.

Before shutting down she checked Ariel's picture again.

The top edge of the newspaper was visible behind his head, though very dark. She zoomed in and read the page title: *The Daily Express.*

It sounded national. She tracked along the line of text, chasing it to the edge of the picture. And read: *Wednesday, 30th November* 1977.

16

Ariel's mouth was dry and bitter. His shirt was damp and stuck to something; but pulling away brought a chill, and he quickly pressed himself back.

A gust rattled the window.

When he finally opened an eye he saw Gretchen asleep beside him. Perspiration stuck them together. Newsprint crunched as he tried to pull away; it was littered with enough hair for a barber-shop floor, and when he touched his ears they were naked. Gretchen's hair was also gone: she wore a lank bob, barely past her jaw. One big ear stuck out like a snail. The scent of hot sleep made him nauseous.

As his last wakeful memories crawled to mind he shivered and paused, hardly breathing. Gretchen either had a breathtaking talent or she was not of the same flesh as him. The human mind is constantly at work rationalising its position, upholding the biases of its user. It does its work by erasing or changing inconvenient facts, by cutting into clean expected narratives the scenes that play before the eyes.

But Ariel's mind had given up. It had clocked off. On its shop floor he found the last attempted cut, a link to the muscle-relaxant pills he had swallowed. But the mind and he both knew they couldn't account for what he had seen. It meant he was on his own.

Far out in a place where nobody could help him.

Arteries fired up. He was getting out. Tonight, right now. If the problem wouldn't respond to classical rules he would use quantum rules, any rules – and if they didn't work he would break them.

The curtains were open; it was dark outside. As his last moments filtered back he sat up and looked around, grabbed his head, felt his neck. It was like waking after death. He inched off the bed. She didn't stir. Her knees were up against her chest, her backbone rising sideways in a spiky cordillera.

It was ten to seven in the evening. He went to the corner of the room and leant watching Gretchen. What species of creature, what phenomenon she was, he couldn't say. But her powers were strong and abandoned.

As he watched, something flashed in her hand.

The phone. Only then did he recall Zeva's voice. It had seemed objective, another of Gretchen's ventriloquisms – but if they were snatches from life it meant that Gretchen had been in contact with Zeva on her phone. And Zeva was in pain.

Ariel's problems were suddenly greater than being surrounded by police. Now he knew Gretchen was the dominant obstacle in herself. She ruled the bubble, and had surrounded it with forces from the real classical world. Forces wielding powers that would destroy him. But perhaps, he thought, if he could grasp even some of her rules – she might also be his principal aid.

He marshalled all the facts he could. In the classical world there was no reason why her phone would have a signal and his not — if anything his phone was much newer — but that was how it was. Now he saw why the family had been reluctant to disturb her on his first night. He cast his mind back, fishing for other patterns; and what came to mind were Margot's persistent references to quantum mechanics. She made no concrete points with them, rather it was as if she were feeling him out, testing his disposition. But it was a strange subject for a woman of Margot's ilk to be conversant with.

He should have chased it further.

More immediately, Ariel realised he should act while Gretchen slept. He held his breath and knelt beside the bed. Sliding a hand beside hers, over the course of a minute he matched her fingers to his, and tried to prise them back.

She snatched the phone down without waking.

Then floorboards groaned outside. Ariel went to the door and slipped out before anyone could find them together.

'Good evening,' Rob puffed off the stairs. 'Just coming to remove your tray.'

'Thank you.' Ariel moved towards him. 'But I haven't finished. I can bring it later.'

'Well, it'll be stone cold. While the kitchen's open I can swap it for sandwiches and crisps if you like, for later? You'll not want stale food sitting around.'

'Really, it's fine. I wonder if you can take me to the manager? I have a question.'

'Oh?' Rob paused. 'I hope everything's satisfactory?'

'Fine, fine.' Ariel made for the stairs.

'But if you could fetch the tray, I'd appreciate it,' said Rob. 'We've had issues.'

Voices hissed over the dining-room floor as they stepped off the stairs. Leonard was standing in the reception arch. He spied Rob and Ariel in the far corridor. 'Ah! Dear boy,' he waved. 'G and Ts, won't you join us? Robert, we'll need some lemon.'

The game had spun again. Ariel couldn't guess why. But if he was going to make a break he needed all the friends he could get. He needed to watch and learn fast.

Leonard swayed over the parquetry to take his arm. 'Bit precipitated this morning, old chum. The things one says under pressure! Hope there's no harm done?' He walked Ariel towards the lounge like a pensioner with his beloved.

Ariel shook his head. 'It was strong, Leonard. Did the police finish their enquiry?'

'Far as I know we're still surrounded. A mystery. But Gretchen is a drama queen, God knows. I said as much to the police but who knows what she's told them. Personally I don't think you were even there. She may have concocted the whole thing.'

'I said I was there. I tried to bandage her, that was all.'

'She just didn't think her story through. Preposterous, from start to finish.'

'No, Leonard — I was there. I only tried to bandage her.' Ariel stopped. He waited for Leonard to turn and accept the point.

'I mean honestly. You're only trying to get to Holland, for God's sake! Probably sick of the sight of us! Probably think we're bloody barking!' Leonard's eyes grew round. He launched into a rocking laugh and pulled Ariel close by his sleeve. 'The thing I've always found, upon reflection, is that the obvious answer isn't often the right one. Don't you find?' He escorted him to the salon's doors.

'I'm a scientist, Leonard. Obvious is good.'

Smoke emptied from the salon in a rolling surf.

'My lovely boy!' came a cry from the fireplace. 'Come to Margot.'

Ariel found her more shrunken this evening, strangely so. Her wig was gone, her make-up was rudimentary and badly applied. As he leant in he smelt age and stale tobacco. 'I thought I was in trouble with you?' he said.

'Oh, for God's sake. Leonard, what did I tell you?' She nuzzled his head. 'Such a sensitive boy. But where's all your hair?'

'Ah.' Ariel pulled back. 'A little change for good luck.'

'Or he's trying to slip through the police line incognito!'

'Ha!' cried Margot. 'Like a spy! So dashing — if only I were ten years younger!'

'You'd want more than bloody ten!' Leonard roared.

As the pair exchanged quips something grew in Ariel's mind. An inkling became a formula, it took shape in a flash. Leonard had given him a key.

It had to do with the personalities in the bubble. Because what failed inside it compared to the outside world were boundaries. The family were fuelled by transgression: of classical laws, of accepted rules and standards. They transgressed for good and bad, and boundaries were open both ways — open for breaching as much as being breached — but to them it was native and they took it as invisible. They felt themselves special cases. Outside laws didn't apply. As transgression invites scrutiny, much of their effort was spent running an immune system. Ariel saw it this morning when a truth they had all witnessed — the girl harming herself — had been rejected.

All creatures strive for acceptance, the most basic social drive. Leonard offering to erase Ariel's meeting with Gretchen was the key. Ariel had been invited into the bubble. The deal was: we won't mention your transgressions if you don't mention ours.

It was as if the family knew they could not be seen. As if there was no chance of their ever facing consequences. As if nothing existed outside these walls.

The bubble was a free animal state. Its membrane was a gloss of words and behaviours that echoed outside norms without reflecting activities inside. It was a rampart. And the immune system protected it at all costs.

Ariel had cracked it. It was the first code.

And something deeper welled inside him: a sense that these were pure humans, simply unregulated by the checks and balances of a society. Doing what humans would do on a desert island: avoid blame and bide time.

Two issues remained on Ariel's worksheet: as an applied scientist he needed a practical key, some switch he could throw in his favour. And as a theoretician he had to face a lurking sense that he was not as separate from the bubble's maths as he liked to think. He even went to the trouble of naming this Issue Three.

It was the big issue: his place in relation to it all.

How conscious the family were of their system remained to be seen. If it was unknown to them it would have different rules than if they operated knowingly. In fact it would have no rules, only momentary compulsions. And if both states were true it would have a different set again, and oscillate between states, creating infinite possibilities. A virtual quantum state, a superposition where a situation could be two things at once.

Ariel's mind went to work behind an affable smile.

'Anyhow.' Leonard's face fell. 'Speaking of police line.'

Margot thrust her wheelchair to the doors. 'I shall make myself bootiful for cocktails. Won't be long. We're having gin and tonics, Harry, just as soon as the lemon appears.'

'Yes, yes,' said Leonard, 'I've put Stan Laurel on the case.' He shut the doors behind Margot, and grew pensive. 'Yes, well: sorry if things were a little frayed. Kids! Who'd have 'em! We'll do it differently tomorrow. Tell them tonight you'll take breakfast with the Borders. They set the places at night, you see. Heaven help who shifts anything, they're worse than bloody automatons.'

There was a knock at the door. Rob came in with a plate of sliced lemon. He turned to Ariel after placing it on the gramophone: 'Will I tell the manager you'd like to see him?'

Ariel glanced at Leonard. He shook his head.

'It's fine – I'll find him later.'

Rob stepped out and pulled the doors shut.

'Set Harry's place with us for the morning!' Leonard boomed after him.

'Well, I can only convey it to management. It's not up to me.'

'You great goose. He'll take his breakfast with the Borders!'

'I can only convey it . . .' Rob's voice faded off.

Leonard gripped Ariel's shoulder: 'A word between friends about Clifford. Not a type you'd want to deal with. Hmm? If I were you I'd keep a distance.' He teetered back, chewing emptily. 'I don't want to besmirch the man. But after a while you get to know people. With me? Undeclared bankrupt, for one thing. And some nasty stories floating about. Unhealthy stories. Not a loved man.'

'He's suddenly very friendly to me.'

'Since he found out you were a doctor. He got you all wrong, see?'

The salon window screeched up. Leonard tossed ice into tumblers, a slice of lemon each, and mixed the drinks half-and-half. 'Police cordon.' He shook his head, glancing back. 'Could be bloody serious. They don't muck about. We're all in that one together. Course — you'll be disadvantaged, being foreign. You won't have access to referees, and visible standing in the community.'

'You think so?' Ariel took his drink.

'Know so. This country's a grid of background information. Within a second they can establish your standing and rule you out. But in your case you've only got us. Of course, we'll do our damnedest, already have. But, well. Village coppers, you know. Frozen-food eaters. They're not going to understand the agenda of a man like you.'

Ariel clinked his glass. The conversation was an introduction to something, he felt himself being manoeuvred. It was the next key. Like an explorer deciphering old pots he saw that the bubble's culture was materialistic in the true anthropological sense. Everything was done to obtain something. All that appeared random was in fact laying a ground, sighting a target, sweetening a pill.

It was a big key. For the first time Ariel could see a horizon. Somehow these subtle keys would open a door to outside. And do it tonight.

With Leonard's next parry he was ready to play.

'I've given thought to your situation,' Leonard sighed up at the ceiling. 'Horrible, and of course we feel partly complicit. You know? Awful mess, and you in a hurry. Hah! When did the police ever take a hurry into account? Much less your village police. All day lazing around outside. Probably a hundred burglaries in town, but what the hell. This is newsworthy. Probably imagine themselves on TV.

Vulnerable young girl, seaside hotel, vicious assault. Anyway, we can't just sit by. I've thought long and hard.'

Ariel wandered a slow circle, eyes down, listening.

'And then it hit me. Bang!' Leonard smacked his brow. 'Consortium. Of course! Connections-wise – bingo! And more importantly,' he raised a finger, 'an instant background. Instant credibility. Local contacts – and all for nothing. All for profit share in the most cutting-edge British project this decade.'

'Wo,' Ariel nodded.

'All for three hundred quid. We can do it now, this instant. Problem solved.'

'Boom. Okay. But I'm not really in a position for investments. You know?'

'You'd be doing us a good turn. Truth is,' his voice fell to a whisper, 'this family falls on my shoulders to care for. If I don't get this project up I may as well hang myself from a lamp post. With me? A last little nudge is all it needs. Then we're home safe. Otherwise – lamp post. May as well. Man's duty. With me?'

'But you know, Leonard – to even start looking at anything financial I would need to go online, and use a phone. So – looks like I don't have an option.'

He lay the bait and sipped his drink. Leonard could go and find Gretchen asleep in his room; in the bubble's altered space-time perception she would be seen to have gone in alone. Ariel was having drinks with Leonard, after all. Before that he was seen with Rob. And most importantly: when Leonard got the phone, it was Ariel's.

He would protect his use of it until Ariel's life was on track and his cab was waiting outside.

'Got it!' Leonard snapped his fingers. 'Why don't I get the phone? Hmm?'

'Well, if Gretchen's up to it. Your call.' Ariel took a slug of gin.

'It's as good as done,' Leonard beamed. 'Won't be a minute.'

17

Ariel went to the gilded cherub on the mantelpiece. He lifted it carefully and found it to be badly moulded plastic. A stamp on the base said *China*. He touched the distressed mirror frame and it was plastic too. Behind a coal scuttle sat a festering plate with baked beans, a dried haemorrhage of ketchup and the coiled brushings of someone's hair.

The bubble was deflating. Light shone into the theatre. All the ropes and pulleys were here, backstage. And he found himself thinking of a bullfight: because he'd heard that by law a bull must be dead within eleven minutes of entering the ring — as this is how long it takes one to learn that his target is not the cape.

He felt a sudden pity that these souls only had a day and a half to strike before their pulleys showed through. Before the cape lost appeal.

A sum came to him as if coded in smoke. What these beings lived for was a feeling that everything was fine. Just that alone. They would break any ethic to achieve it. Logic had no part, neither empathy. They aimed for the feeling – and could generate it against any evidence. Their immune system existed to destroy any clue that it wasn't genuine. And as generating the feeling called for destroying more ethics, it became harder to face and required more of the feeling. A cycle.

Ariel let the idea roam his mind. He applied the template to the world at large, the new society. A knot grew in his gut. He applied it to his world of machine intelligence – and saw that he may or may not achieve it; but it didn't matter.

Because he would say that he had; and nobody alive could disprove it.

His flywheels flew off their axles. Issue Three

came down to a simple sum. If tonight is the evidence, he thought, then the world is not designing machines like humans. It's designing humans like machines. Virtual people.

As he thought this he looked over at the window drapes. 'Hey,' he addressed the bulge. 'God of war.'

'Hey.' Jack's furry ears popped out.

'Everyone forgets you're there. You must hear everything.'

'They know I don't listen.'

'A-ha. And don't you listen?'

'Yeah. Sometimes it's better than the game.'

The doors flew open. Clifford bustled in. 'Oh *please!*' He rushed to the windows, throwing them up like cabers. 'Smoke! It's just not on.' He stormed back to the doors, swinging them open and shut, making a bellows of the salon. Ariel watched until a certain number of exhalations was reached, a number known only to Clifford. After which he stopped and approached, clenching and unclenching his hands.

'I promised myself not to say anything – but between us, Doctor, in the best possible way, I wouldn't be spending too much time with this lot.

Well, you've seen for yourself. As your host I felt obliged to say something.'

'Okay. I guess you can't choose your guests.'

Clifford shook his head in despair. '*Guests?* Strictly between us, Doctor, they're squatters. Don't be fooled. They might swan about the place like its masters but they haven't paid for a night here ever. Not once.' He leant in from the waist, fixing a stare on Ariel. 'Do you know what we call them, sir? The *Borgias.*' He let the name sit for a moment, reeking of murderous Renaissance skulduggery. 'The *Borgias*,' he rasped filthily. 'You've seen for yourself why. Do you see the portrait in the hall out there? Of the man?'

'Standing tall, yes.'

'My father. Founded this place with the sweat off his brow.'

'But – can't you just tell them to leave? The police are right here.'

'Not in this country. More rights than the Queen.'

They heard Margot rattling up the hall. 'Do you know, Doctor,' Clifford hurriedly whispered, 'half the fine objects in this hotel are kept under lock and key. Or they go straight into her bag.' He stepped to the door in anticipation, opened it and thrust a finger at the ceiling when she appeared. 'Smoking! What have I said!'

'Up your arse.' Margot rolled in without looking.

Clifford threw a scowl and fumed out.

The wind grew ruthless outside. It rattled windows and whined down the chimney with shudders of ash. Margot turned to Ariel. She was freshly daubed and wore her wig. Her feet were red and scaly, bursting through orthopaedic sandals on the stirrups of her chair. 'Did I tell you, Harry, that there was a reason you were here?'

'Really?' Ariel paced nervously.

'Yes. It has to do with frequencies, particles, waves and time and space. All things you understand.'

'A-ha. Boom.'

Margot tracked him back and forth with her eyes. They shone mistily but with a hardness Ariel hadn't seen before now. 'You don't believe me,' she said.

'Oh, I believe that you believe it. Tell me more.'

'You don't believe in anything but your boring

old what-goes-up-must-come-down classical basket-weaving Newtonian tosh. As simple as bloody Meccano.'

Ariel stopped to face her. 'Actually I don't. But I believe you believe in more – and that's the only question here. I'd love to hear it. My mind is open.'

Margot narrowed her eyes. 'I bring it up because I'm a little surprised to see you still floundering. More than a little surprised, given your mind. All the clues are here. It's all perfectly scientific, you know.'

'Well, Margot – I'd love to hear more. Because it may or may not be.'

Margot's face fell. 'Oh. I thought you were with me.'

'I am with you. But I don't agree that all the clues are scientific.'

'But don't you see? Entanglement! It's been discovered! Certain particles in atomic nuclei are partnered with particles in other atoms any distance away, across the universe even. And more importantly – quantum computers will soon prove entanglement between parallel universes!'

'A-ha. Basic entanglement is true. But that

doesn't suggest it's a lens through which all experience can be interpreted. What I mean is — I don't see how my being grounded overnight at an airport can have many more interpretations than the weather being too bad for flying. And bad weather is simple physics.'

'Oh my God. But Harry! Don't you see — you're not at the airport!'

'Well. You know what I mean. If you're trying to suggest we're in a parallel universe, it would be easier to believe if I hadn't come in a taxi.'

Margot paused to wipe spittle from her mouth with a tissue. 'Dear God, I'm trying to make this so easy.'

'I'll tell you a secret, Margot: part of a thesis I did was about entangled atoms. But it didn't work. You know why? Because in the end I'm an applied scientist and there was no way to bring the idea from theory into practice. Nothing in the classical universe showed the effect of entanglement. If I could see something with my eyes then I could chase it, make a breakthrough and use it. But I couldn't even isolate nuclei in a predictable way. So I had to take it out.'

'Yes! Yes! You see? Oh, Harry! You're so nearly

there, go on, go on – and what does quantum mechanics say about time?'

'In the Everett Interpretation you so love? That it doesn't exist. But look at my watch – it's getting late. That's the applied truth of things.'

Margot slowly deflated in her chair. 'Everyone's just against me these days.' Her face became an artwork of self-pity. She spoke to herself, following each statement with a withering breath. 'Here's me thinking you were with me. Ah, well.'

'I'm not being unreasonable, Margot.'

'It's all right,' she said faintly.

And this quiet, descending scene, where the old woman shrank before his eyes, became bizarre and wizened, was joined by a full-hearted scream from the passage.

A conflict approached. Ariel's heart skipped.

'You'll do as you're bloody told!' barked Leonard.

'Get off me, I'll call the police!' It was Gretchen.

After some scuffling they burst through the doors. Margot's mouth fell open. 'Who gave her scissors!' she yelled.

Gretchen flailed in with scissors in one hand, the phone in the other.

'Give it to me!' roared Leonard.

'Leonard!' cried Margot. 'Don't, she's gone mad! Look at her hair!'

'Give it to me!' Leonard was crimson and shining with sweat.

The girl twisted free in a barrage of blows. She nicked his arm with the scissors. He yelped and she leapt away, pointing the blades at everyone in turn, crouched ready to pounce. She heaved and sneered till all fell quiet, then came to face Ariel, scissors up like a dagger. 'This is what you've done,' she hissed, stabbing her arm and dragging the blades through her flesh.

Leonard leapt at her, snatching up the scissors and pelting them over the piano.

'Go to hell!' she screamed.

'As long as you're around I'm already there!'

'Shh, Leonard,' hissed Margot. 'That's not the way.'

'*I wish she'd been a bloody abortion!*' he yelled back.

Gretchen stood shaking, skin hanging ragged from her arm. 'I *am* an abortion,' she cried, and ran sobbing from the room.

'Well, that's just what I bloody need!' shouted Margot. 'Thank you, Harry, thank you, Leonard. You've no empathy at all. That's not the way to do things.'

'We need the bloody phone!' barked Leonard. 'Don't you understand? You can't sit there day after bloody day badgering for progress if you won't let me chase it! We could have been secure by now if you hadn't hampered every bloody thing I've done! You're like a virus! You're a pollutant! All you do is pollute!'

Margot let out a howl. It had a hysterical edge, the falsetto of someone tossed by a car. 'Where are my pills?' She fussed for her bag. 'Oh God.'

'Yes, reach for your pills! Let me find you a bloody funnel!'

She howled again, a climbing wail. 'I was only trying to help. I'm just an old woman, I'm not strong enough for this. I was only trying to be compassionate.'

'Oh yes, well, bloody marvellous!' Leonard screamed. 'What would you have done with the scissors? Called a bloody guru to waft them out of her hand!'

'I would've got the game off Jack and swapped it for the phone. I don't know why you're all against me. I'll not trouble you much longer.'

Leonard paced noisily, fists clenched by his sides. 'If you'd have given me a bloody minute I would've gotten there!' He gathered new force. 'If you hadn't jumped in at the last minute and spoilt everything we would've been fine!' Over her howls he stormed to the curtain and ripped it back. 'Give me the game.'

'Get lost,' mumbled Jack.

'Give it to me! Now!'

'Don't hurt him!' Margot shrieked. 'He's all I've got left in the world! Stay away from him!' She wheeled herself over in a frenzy, butting Leonard aside and almost flattening the boy. He crouched over his game screen, unmoving.

'Has he had his Ritalin?' Leonard snapped.

'Of course! He may have had it twice, I can never tell with the state you have me in.' Margot pulled alongside and reached for the game. Jack slapped her away. When she tackled him he spun round and pushed the chair with all his force.

'No!' The boy flew at her, raining blows. 'I hate you!' he screamed. 'I hate you!'

Ariel stood throbbing with current. When Margot began to lose the fight he tried to get between them. The boy was a cyclone. As his blows connected further up her body and finally her head, Ariel drew back his arm and swatted him across the floor.

Jack lay stunned. His fuzzy ears twitched askew.

Leonard stood quaking over him. In one ferocious swoop he snatched the game and flung it across the room. It flew into the fire, tossing up a cloud of tiny fireworks.

Jack ran squealing to it.

Margot seemed to inflate in her chair, her features growing large and grotesque. Raw power shimmered off her. As Ariel watched, the strap of a sandal blew off her foot with a crack and a puff of skin.

It was a derationalised zone, of forces from the edge of nature.

Margot thrust herself through the doors and out. 'I can't take any more!'

Leonard stood taking stock. He glowered at Ariel and eventually rose off his heels to yell, 'Look what you've done to our family!'

Ariel levelled a gaze, watched him wipe his chin. Then turned and walked away. Acids of frustration and rage had reached too frightening a pitch. They threatened to break him for ever. From the stairs he heard Margot howling outside, her voice whipped round by the wind.

Passing room twelve he threw himself at the door like a battering ram. It didn't budge. He went up to his room, gathered his bags and walked down the stairs for the last time. The police could arrest him. Prison would be preferable. He was destroyed as it was. Gretchen's face appeared through an inch of her doorway as he passed. He flew at her, roaring, and she slammed it shut.

Olivia appeared on the next landing. She was just there, arms wrapped around herself, looking out from the shadows. 'Psst,' she hissed. 'I've got a plan.'

Ariel didn't slow. 'So have I.'

'No, no – seriously.'

'So have I. Seriously.' He stepped past her.

'There's a car.' She followed, clutching at him. 'Our car's here. Outside!'

'And you just thought of this? After a day you just remembered you had a car?'

'Let's go out there now, just the two of us! It's a madhouse, Ari.'

'What's the cost?' The pair reached the dining room. Ariel strode on, dragging her by the tips of her grasping fingers.

'There's no cost! Take me with you. Let's start again, somewhere else, without all this. From scratch!'

'Start what again?' he said flatly. 'Show me the keys.'

She fumbled in her cardigan pocket, pulling out a crumpled tissue and a pair of keys. Ariel opened the front door and stood back. She squinted into the night.

They stepped out together.

Behind the building, in a cutting between the hotel and Clifford's cottage, an old Rover sat listing in the rain. Olivia's hand trembled as she pointed a key at the door. Then the keys fell. Ariel scooped them out of the wet and wrenched the driver's door open. He held it for her but she paused, head down, for no reason.

'So?' he prompted.

She slid behind the wheel and took the keys. When he was beside her she sat without moving.

It was a heavy old car, smelling of must and leather. Still it shook in the gusts that swept between buildings.

'Does it start?' Ariel snapped.

She didn't answer but sat perfectly still, looking into her lap. He saw her shoulders begin to tremble, then her head. She hissed from her throat and broke into a sob. Ariel slumped impatiently. He'd seen so much crying in the last day, from every point on the spectrum – but he saw that this was something new, an involuntary jerking, a hysteria. He knew she was unable to drive the car. He sighed and put a hand to her shoulder.

'I told you there were things you should know,' she wept. 'This all could've been so graceful and elegant without bloody Gretchen Malkin.'

Ariel watched her. 'Why does that name sound familiar?'

'She's the taxi driver's girl.'

Ariel's gaze narrowed to nothing. From far back in his mind he retrieved a snapshot, clipped to a dashboard, of a lanky grinning girl. A son the father never had.

He turned Olivia's face towards him. 'Why is she here?'

'We rescued her.' Olivia turned away.

'From what?' Ariel tried to catch her eye. 'Olivia
— from what?'

When she turned she could barely form words.
She looked up, imploring with her eyes, as if
approaching a border they could not return from.
'She was murdered. He stabbed her forty-one times
in the back for having menstruated.'

Rain pattered over the car. The air grew icy.

A weight settled in Ariel. He sat watching Olivia;
and grew heavy. When he looked around him,
across the rainswept ground and the hulk of the
Cliffs, his movements were slow and smooth. 'Why
did she come here?' he whispered.

'The body was in the boot of his car. He
brought her to dump in the sea. Thankfully he
then drove up the coast a few miles to shoot
himself.'

Ariel sat quiet for a minute. Then he slowly
opened the door and stepped out.

Olivia scrambled out as if bitten. 'Please
don't go.'

He frowned and walked from the car.

Waves boomed over the bluff, dousing them
with spray as they neared the front of the building.

Reaching the steps, he took her hand and guided her up to the door. 'Take care of yourself,' he said. She huddled half inside, their eyes met for a moment. He pecked her cheek and gently pushed her in, closing the glass door.

She fell away from him into a murky green like a corpse fading into the deep.

18

Breakers banged over the boat ramp. Light from the dining-room window captured their spray in swirls and jags. Below on the narrow descent to the ramp Margot was sitting stiff in the wheelchair, head bobbing around in the gale.

Down the track the night was cut through with flashing vehicles and dazzling floodlights. Ariel counted three police cars, and now saw flashing amber lights, auxiliaries of some kind. Forms in heavy rain gear milled around. Just beyond the surf, two barges lit the water pearly grey.

Ariel stopped. He took his bags off his shoulder and leant them under the dining-room window.

He could see Margot's contours in the light, and came down towards her. To his right the boat ramp rose from the sea like a tongue.

Two hunched figures rounded the corner behind him.

'Off swimming, Margot?' Clifford yelled. Rob stopped two paces behind him.

Margot wheeled herself on to the ramp. The body of the sea crashed towards her. She trembled with the strain of the incline as she locked the chair's brake.

'Off you go!' yelled Clifford. 'And good riddance.'

'You're all against me! Stay back!'

'We *are* against you, Margot. This property was left to me and you have made a mission of its destruction. You're a destroyer. Nobody here will miss you.'

'He didn't leave a will!'

'He didn't have to leave a will! It's clear which one of us was left a hotel to run! And which one was fit for an asylum!'

'He was my father too!' She broke down. After a moment she looked up and saw Ariel bent under his hood.

'He used to stand at the top of those stairs,

Harry, and say that he wished me dead. He used to stand on the landing you stood on, in front of the door you've just used, and say, "Useless girl."' Her face crumpled. 'How could I be any different, when I've not been properly raised? How could I? We're living our truth. We're not hiding. We're being what we can. It's still a family.'

Ariel didn't move. He was touched by the sea's nature, reaching over its edges with pulling hands, intent on snatching things in. Like death itself, the sea stretched out for them, hissing.

Margot sat shaken by the wind. An immense pity washed through Ariel. He saw an old uncared-for child, simply waiting for someone to say she'd be fine.

She looked up plaintively. 'I have a right to exist!'

Clifford turned and walked away. Rob followed, glancing back. 'I'd best set the places for breakfast,' he said. 'The Borgias will need it after this gala turn.'

Ariel looked up at the hotel. It seemed to shimmer in the storm. He gazed for a moment before turning back to the wretched form on the ramp.

'You have something to tell me,' he called. 'Before I leave.'

'I tried to make it easy for you, Harry. But like all you bloody scientists your mind is a closed door.' She reversed the chair off the ramp and wheeled around to face him.

He looked down, nodding. 'Are you dead?' he finally asked.

'Do I look bloody dead?' She jangled her arms about. 'I've changed, that's all. Do you agree that humans have a frequency? That television has a frequency? That through the right receivers they're as solid as each other? It's so bloody obvious, Harry.'

'What you're saying is you're dead. And if I believe you – why then, if you have the freedom of frequencies, are you here fighting each other in this hell?'

'It's what we were doing. It's what we can do. You didn't think we'd turn into angels with bloody harps? Is that how you imagine it? To think you were designing intelligent machines when you can't even get your head around this!'

'I don't see why I had to be any part of it.' He prepared to walk away.

She wheeled back up the path as Ariel bent

into the wind above her, clothes cracking like sails. The black around Margot was deepened by spray in the light. Then, looking up, he saw flickering in the hotel windows.

He ran a step towards the building. Smoke billowed from the rear in massive clouds. Through the dining room he saw rolling balls of flame, swirls of heat that consumed all around them.

In a top-storey window, Olivia stood looking down.

He ran to the steps, then stopped and stared down the track. The area was swarming with emergency services. There were also workers of some kind, heavy-set men in rain gear. Among the vehicles were also some tractors, and now a crane on a flatbed truck swung a boom over the water. He set off sprinting towards the first officers he could see.

Flying at the first group of men, he pointed back to the hotel. 'Fire!' he yelled.

The officers sauntered past him. 'Derek's got a winch,' said one.

'Right you are, I'll grab me gloves,' said another.

Ariel clutched at the man's arm – and felt nothing.

He stood staring at his hand. When he looked back he saw Margot nearly upon him. Her chair seemed to wheel itself.

He slumped.

'I'm sorry, darling.' She drew up beside him. 'Bloody Jack's set alight to the curtains. Let's just say yours wasn't the only commemoration we geared up for this week. Though of course we would have laid on a spread just for you. We've barely had a fisherman through in the last year. Anyway. I'll put drama aside for a moment and do the right thing. We had such a nice time planned for you.'

Ariel retched into the dirt. 'Are we all dead?'

'You poor thing.' She took his hand and gently pulled him to the water's edge.

Men bustled around and through them, going about their business. She stroked his hand and threw her gaze at a commotion between a barge and the crane on the shore. Ariel followed it.

A painted red bird appeared, wavering underwater then bursting up with a hiss, turning on its chains. It was the tail fin of an aircraft. Squinting through the glare Ariel saw cushions and luggage floating in behind it, sucked by its extraction from the sea.

He turned to Margot.

'Scattered between here and Stansted,' she said. 'Hell of a bang. But it's all in the past now, darling. It's just low-frequency junk.'

'This is where the quantum talk was heading,' he whispered.

'Well, give us some credit, we've never rescued a scientist before. Where was I to begin? It was all going to be so lovely. But of course, the best-laid plans of mice and men. All you should know is that love is the bridge between the living and the dead. Nobody thinks about it, but every investment of feeling between souls is nothing more than a commitment to look upon the lifeless corpse of the other. Do you see? Death is all there truly is. The only for ever. And that fleeting organic time, half of which we spend in the bloody toilet, is as insignificant as the random passage of a fly. That, my love, is true science.'

Ariel quietly wept under his hood.

'You will remain entangled with those you love. Time may seem long to them but it will pass in a flash for you. That's where quantum comes in. Not to mention the molecular science. Do you agree that atoms have weight? That they cannot be created or destroyed, merely changed in form? That the human body is known to lose twenty-one grams of weight upon death? Those grams are you. Without hideous carbons, or stagnant water. Obviously I'll have a few more, with make-up.'

Ariel looked up into the dark. 'But why here?'

'It's where you crossed over. Nothing too astounding, darling – why do you think spectres roam their spots? You don't see Anne Boleyn on the New York subway, for God's sake, though I suppose she'd be free to go.'

'But – why? What are you all doing?'

'Exactly what we were doing when we came over.'

'So – what will I be doing?'

'What are you doing now?'

'Trying to get the hell out of here.'

'There you go then.'

Ariel pondered this, and felt a shiver. He broke off and made for the road.

'Oh I see, we're not good enough for you!' she spat. 'You came to rest with some fractured souls and feel yourself above them! What soul did you ever fix in your life? What thing did you ever truly give to anyone? What service did you perform? You've done nothing but please yourself. Pride yourself. If you thought death had no spiritual meaning, perhaps you're wrong. Perhaps this is it. Look at all the people in this building who accept you. Love you. You scorn them because they haven't the right meat on their bones, haven't the right notions in their heads. Why don't you put some meat on them? Why don't you feed them, fill them, patch their wounds? If you have never done it before, if you have always chased the healthy, the independent, the carefree — then how could you expect to come anywhere but here? You selfish child! All you've done is invent machines to keep us apart, to lessen empathy. All you've done is devote yourself to the strong and the blithe. And look what you've left in your wake. Whole masses of souls just like us! This, Harry, is what you've earned. It's what you've built, using all your intelligence. Is it hell? Are we hell? Or are *you* hell? Hell is your self, Harry Panic. Go and bloody tweet that.'

Beyond the furthest gang of workers Ariel could see no land. All was black. He hung his head and came back to Margot. She sat watching intently, gauging his mood.

'Come.' She held out a hand. 'It's early days.'

They moved back up the track towards the building and its flames, now licking eaves. Leonard was on the steps with the phone to his ear.

'It's not on!' he shouted. 'If this is to go through we need all hands on deck. It'll make all our names!'

Ariel peered up at the top window. Gretchen stood smiling down. He made to enter the building, rugging himself against the flames. Then he paused, and stepped back.

Margot guessed his thoughts: 'She'll come here to remember you — I promise.'

'But she won't see me?'

'Well, you are fresh off the boat, as we say — and fog can help. We'll see what we can do. Get some drinks into her.'

'*Drinks?*'

'Why not, darling?' Margot pointed him up the steps. 'We're not called spirits for bloody nothing.'

19

The driver kept one eye on his screen as Zeva's coordinates approached. 'Bierstone Inlet,' he muttered. 'Must be. Bad night for it, storm's just passed and there's fog due in a bit. You picked some time for the seaside.'

'Yeah. I kind of guessed I wouldn't need luggage.'

The car left the main road and curled around bends like a fox's snout in a story. Zeva was lost in herself, watching treetops quiver under a moon. Rain streamed in sheets around corners before them, seeming to follow the road without spilling.

As if trapped by all this, she pulled out her phone.

The signal was gone.

Raw voltage inside her had grown over the course of the day. Now she was numb. She peered into the darkness, trying to judge the shape of the land. The air smelt fresh. The last building they passed was a huge resort perched on the coast, and she craned to watch it fall behind them.

'Not that one.' The driver saw her watching. 'Easy mistake to make, but we're going to the other side of the inlet, few miles yet.'

She checked her screen again: no signal.

The car hit gravel and slowed.

Ahead beside the road a blitz of obstruction lights, police cars and salvage equipment stretched for a hundred yards or more. The area could have been an international border for the amount of floodlit activity.

'Bugger.' The driver pointed. 'I reckon the spot you want's about two hundred yards past that lot. I doubt we'll get in, though.'

An officer wandered over when he saw the cab slow. He shook his head, motioning the obvious, and waved them on.

'It's definitely here somewhere.' Zeva squinted as they pulled away. 'Can you just drop me, like up ahead at the rise there? I can try going over the top.'

'If you're sure,' said the driver. 'I'll be a bit further up, there's a lay-by in half a mile, if you can make your way back?'

'Fine,' she said. 'Let's settle the bill. If I'm not back in half an hour you can go.'

Leaving the car, she scrambled up the rise and searched the other side. Fog was gathering on the water, and she saw she wasn't far from the recovery camp. She stood facing a pair of tractors with trailers below her. Still there were fewer people nearby, and it was darker. She followed one stray band of light as she made her way down the slope.

Then a man saw her, and stepped into her path. 'Oi!' he called. 'No spectators, you don't want to be round here.' He was gnarled and ruddy like a farmer, and one of few on the site without high-visibility gear, as if he were a local volunteer.

Zeva tried her charm. 'I'm sorry,' she smiled. 'I'm looking for a place that must be further along the coast. I figured it's easier to navigate by the beach.'

'Ain't nothing past here.' The man folded his arms. 'Nature reserve if you go any further, but that'll put you miles out of Bierstone. Where is it you're looking for?'

'A guesthouse along here somewhere. I guess it's on the sea.'

'No, no, my love, nothing along here for miles now.'

'But I have good information. Maybe I'll just go look, it must be here.'

'Telling you, my love, look around. Flat as the eye can see. There was a place used to stand over there on the bluff, the Cliffs Hotel. But long gone now, burnt down in the seventies. I'm sorry, darlin'; wrong track altogether.'

Zeva's heart sank. 'Okay. But will you tell anyone if I walk along the beach in the other direction? I travelled a long way for this.'

He considered it, looking around. 'Just make sure you don't come back this far. That's the Boston flight they're pulling out of the water and it's not a pretty sight.'

Zeva's numbness served her a few minutes more. Then she found the remains of an old concrete path along the bluff, just a fragment; and below it what might once have been a boat ramp. She settled on it looking out to sea.

Her heart finally broke. The material truth was before her. Classical physics had failed his plane. She felt the dam-burst inside and knew it was her essence, her innocence and freedom that emptied through her eyes.

Within an hour the fog had swallowed the universe around her. Suddenly her life seemed only to span the last year, the time when Ariel's words filled her screen, her heart and mind. Her phone had pinged only hours before, and she had thought he was there. But now she checked the screen, and it was dead.

She fumbled to his picture; it was black.

Ariel wasn't there. Nobody was there.

She was truly alone.

Zeva lost track of the time she spent on the bluff. Maybe she dozed. Maybe she became absent in some other way. However it was, she jumped when a voice rang out:

'*Mein Gott!*' it gasped. 'It's the young Jackie Onassis.'

'Steady on,' came a man's voice.

Zeva spun round to see a stern Victorian pile loom out of the mist behind her. Light shone under a portico. The man tottered down, beaming heartily. 'Bred into the British, this love of the sea,' he said. 'Though I think you've taken it a tad too far.'

'God,' Zeva stood, 'I was a million miles away.'

'What else is there to do? Bloody weather. We've been forced into a stupor, a sort of induced coma, while it all passes.'

'Not a coma, Leonard, for God's sake,' said a woman behind him.

'I'm sorry.' Zeva brushed herself off. 'I didn't mean to trespass.'

'Nonsense. G and Ts inside, won't you join us?' The man waved her to the steps.

'Thank you so much. Then I really need to find a way out of here. Do you ever get a phone signal?'

About Hammer

Hammer is the most well-known film brand in the UK, having made over 150 feature films which have been terrifying and thrilling audiences worldwide for generations.

Whilst synonymous with horror and the genre-defining classics it produced in the 1950s to 1970s, Hammer was recently rebooted in the film world as the home of "Smart Horror", with the critically acclaimed *Let Me In* and *The Woman in Black*. With *The Woman in Black: Angel of Death* scheduled for 2015, Hammer has been re-born.

Hammer's literary legacy is also now being revived through its new partnership with Arrow Books. This series features original novellas by some of today's most celebrated authors, as well as classic stories from nearly a century of production.

In 2014 Hammer Arrow published books by DBC Pierre, Lynne Truss and Joanna Briscoe as well as a novelisation of the forthcoming *The Woman in Black: Angel of Death*, continuing a programme that began with bestselling novellas from Helen Dunmore and Jeanette Winterson. Beautifully produced and written to read in a single sitting, Hammer Arrow books are perfect for readers of quality contemporary fiction.

For more information on Hammer
visit: www.hammerfilms.com or
www.facebook.com/hammerfilms